The
GRIFFIN
of DARKWOOD

BECKY CITRA

COTEAU BOOKS

Edited by Kathryn Cole
Book designed by Tania Craan
Typeset by Susan Buck
Cover image regulus56 / photocase.com
Printed and bound in Canada

Library and Archives Canada Cataloguing in Publication

Citra, Becky, author
    The griffin of Darkwood / Becky Citra.

Issued in print and electronic formats.
ISBN 978-1-55050-691-4 (paperback).--ISBN 978-1-55050-692-1 (pdf).--
ISBN 978-1-55050-693-8 (epub).--ISBN 978-1-55050-694-5 (mobi)

    I. Title.

PS8555.I87G75 2016   jC813'.54   C2016-903551-4
                                            C2016-903552-2

Library of Congress Control Number   2016941701

2517 Victoria Avenue
Regina, Saskatchewan
Canada S4P 0T2
www.coteaubooks.com

10 9 8 7 6 5 4 3 2 1

Available in Canada from:
Publishers Group Canada
2440 Viking Way
Richmond, British Columbia
Canada V6V 1N2

Available in the US from:
Orca Book Publishers
www.orcabook.com
1-800-210-5277

Coteau Books gratefully acknowledges the financial support of its publishing program by: the Saskatchewan Arts Board, The Canada Council for the Arts, the Government of Saskatchewan through Creative Saskatchewan, the City of Regina. We further acknowledge the [financial] support of the Government of Canada. Nous reconnaissons l'appui [financier] du gouvernement du Canada.

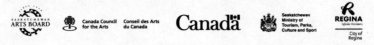

To my sister Janet

chapter one

THE LAST CHAPTER

)

WILL POPPY PEERED THROUGH the window at a figure in a long black coat and purple boots marching up the front walk of their brick block of flats. She was carrying a white square box.

"Oh, no!" he said. "It's Aunt Mauve."

"Not today," whispered his mother, Adrienna. She was sitting at a wobbly round table covered with papers. "I can't bear it today."

The old elevator wheezed and thumped in the hallway.

"I'll make her go!" said Will.

"No," said Adrienna. "After all, she is our only living relative. Family is family, William."

"But we're writing, Mum. She can't come when we're writing."

The doorbell rang.

Will opened the door and gaped at Aunt Mauve. A dozen sleek brown heads dangled from a fur cape around her neck, and a dozen pairs of black glass eyes glinted at him. The cape smelled like mothballs, and worn patches poked through the scruffy fur.

"They're squirrels." Aunt Mauve thrust the white box at Will. "A cake for your tea." She twirled on her purple boots.

"How thoughtful," murmured Adrienna.

Will rolled his eyes. He lifted the edge of the lid. Inside was a tiny round cake the colour of canned peas. He jabbed it with his finger. Hard as a rock. Another of Aunt Mauve's bargains. Aunt Mauve was as poor as Will and his mother.

Why was she trying to be nice all of a sudden?

Aunt Mauve sidled over to the table. Her sharp brown eyes peered over Adrienna's shoulder. "You must be feeling better. You're working on your book."

"I've had a good day," said Adrienna. "My breathing is better. I'm sure it was just some kind of flu bug."

"What do you want?" said Will. He looked longingly at his writing book on the couch. He'd been working on a battle scene between the Knights of Valour and the Knights of Death.

"I don't want anything," said Aunt Mauve. "That's a fine thank you for bringing you the cake."

She turned to Adrienna. "How many chapters left to go?"

"One," said Adrienna.

"And your publisher, Mr. Barnaby, believes it will make you rich?" Aunt Mauve's eyes glinted.

"Oh, Mauve, not rich! Maybe a little money to help us out. But that's not why I write. I write because I love it. Will's writing a book, too. He's a born writer."

Aunt Mauve snorted. "Children don't write. Well, ta-ta, then. I'm off to a party."

Will didn't believe her for one second. Who would invite someone as awful as Aunt Mauve to a party? As soon as the elevator started its groaning descent, he said, "I hate her! And why is she hanging around us now? She never bothered with us until you started writing your book."

"You should try to like her," said Adrienna. "After all..."

Will sighed. "She's our only living relative."

He checked out the window to see if Aunt Mauve had really gone. His aunt was sailing down the walk, her squirrels swinging wildly. A little man in a tidy grey suit squeezed past her. "Mr. Barnaby's here," said Will.

"Goodness, this is our day for visitors," said Adrienna. "Maybe he's bringing good news!"

❖

Oliver Barnaby was the owner of Barnaby Book Publishers Inc. on Oxford Street in London. He perched on the couch beside Adrienna and held her thin hand. "My dear Adrienna, do I dare ask?"

Adrienna smiled faintly. "I'm writing the last chapter tonight."

"Excellent, excellent. I've been waiting for it. We're almost ready to go to the printer." Mr. Barnaby rubbed his hands through his snowy hair.

"William dear," said Adrienna. "Make Mr. Barnaby some tea."

Will boiled the kettle in the kitchen and put out the teapot and three chipped cups. Bits of conversation drifted from the other room.

"You're looking rather pale, my dear. Are you taking care of yourself?"

"I'm fine," said Adrienna. "Perhaps I'm not sleeping as well as I should. It must be excitement over the book."

"I see the lift's been fixed. That must be a relief."

"Oh, yes. Climbing five flights of stairs was too much

for me. I got quite winded."

The kettle whistled, and Will missed the rest. When he carried in the tea tray, Adrienna said, "Mr. Barnaby was just telling me how much interest there is in my book."

"I predict a runaway bestseller," said Mr. Barnaby. "The fantasy market is huge."

"You're an optimist, Oliver," said Adrienna.

Mr. Barnaby flushed. "Nevertheless, it will give you some income."

"Of course, we'll give some of the money to Aunt Mauve," said Adrienna.

Will groaned.

"She is your father's sister, Will."

Mr. Barnaby leaned closer to Adrienna. "Have you settled on the title?"

"The Magical Night."

"Yes! Yes! Perfect."

Adrienna Poppy and Will had great faith in Mr. Barnaby. Teacups clinked.

✧

Adrienna settled herself at the round table with ten sheets of clean lined paper and her box of pencils. The box was royal blue with the words *100 PENCILS* in maroon block letters across the top. She had bought it in a cluttered little stationery shop called *Abracadabra* on Knight Street. The pencils were purple and were covered with tiny sparkling stars. Adrienna called them her magic pencils.

One thousand pages, one hundred chapters, a chapter each week...and one pencil for every chapter. As the manuscript grew, the pencils disappeared until there was only one left in the box. Adrienna took it out now. "My Muse is calling me," she said.

Adrienna's Muse inspired her to write. The Muse was from Ancient Greece. She wore a long white dress and a wreath of green leaves in her hair, and only Adrienna could see her.

"Hey, my Muse is calling me too!" said Will. He remembered how amazing it had been the first time he'd seen his Muse. He'd been writing a poem at school (he'd been stuck on the words and sweat had broken out on his forehead), and then a knight had clanked up the aisle and stood right beside him. The knight removed a visor and Will stared into the green eyes of a girl with cascading hair. None of the other kids had noticed a thing, but Will had figured it out right away. He'd been waiting for his Muse for a long time. The last verse of the poem was a breeze to write.

The Muses didn't always come when Adrienna and Will wrote. Most of the time they had to struggle on their own. But now both Muses were here. Will sat on the sofa with his writing book propped open against his knees. His novel had grown to a satisfying forty pages. It was the fifth novel he had started, and this one he vowed to finish. Beginnings were easy. He had hundreds of ideas. Finishing was the hard part.

He and his mother wrote and wrote. When the sky outside grew dark, Will tiptoed to the kitchen, warmed up some chicken soup and crept off to bed.

At midnight, Adrienna put down the pencil. The next morning, she was asleep when Will got up. There was a brown envelope with Mr. Barnaby's name on the front lying on the table. Will peeked inside. Chapter One

Hundred of *The Magical Night*.

Clutching the envelope, he raced along the cold deserted streets to the office of Barnaby Book Publishers Inc. and banged on the narrow black door. Mr. Barnaby wasn't there. He waited for ten minutes and then pushed the envelope through the brass post slot.

He ran the rest of the way to school.

�֍

When Will got home from school, Mrs. Ginny, who lived in the flat below them, was waiting on the walk. Tears streamed down her cheeks. "She's gone, Will. Your mother's gone."

"Gone where?" asked Will.

"Oh, Will...she's dead, luv."

"She...she...can't be!" Will stammered. "She wasn't even sick." He thought about his mother struggling up the stairs. "Well, maybe a little sick. But she was getting better. She told me so!"

"My poor wee lad." Mrs. Ginny folded Will in her arms.

She tucked Will into the bed in her spare room with a hot water bottle and a cup of hot tea, because he was freezing all over.

That night, Will cried himself to sleep.

✖

On a cold wet morning in early April, a handful of mourners huddled under huge black umbrellas at the cemetery – Aunt Mauve, looking like a crow in her black coat, Father Jim from the church, a very pale Mr. Barnaby, Mrs. Ginny and Mr. Manley from the corner shop.

Will stood beside Aunt Mauve. "I hope you're not

going to blubber," she hissed. "You're twelve years old. Not a baby!"

That was only the second thing Aunt Mauve had said to him at the cemetery. The first was, "Did your mother finish the book?"

Will held his eyes wide open and forced back his tears. He had already cried so hard he felt like a scraped out pumpkin. And he had no intention of giving his aunt the satisfaction of seeing him cry now. He glanced around and spotted a woman wearing a long white dress and a wreath of green leaves and a knight in shiny armour, standing beside a tree. The Muses! He had never seen his mother's Muse before, but he knew right away that it was her. He stared hard and then, when he blinked, they were gone.

By the time Father Jim had finished reading from the book of services, the drizzle had turned to steady rain. Aunt Mauve's lips turned blue as she looked up the street.

A black taxi pulled over to the side of the road and Aunt Mauve grabbed Will's arm. "Pick up your feet! No dawdling! You're coming with me!"

Will tried to twist out of her grasp. He had felt numb throughout the whole service and he hadn't said a word to anyone. "I have to talk to Mr. Barnaby!" he cried.

Aunt Mauve's nails tightened like claws.

"But Mr. Barnaby said –" The next thing Will knew, he was inside the taxi with the door slammed shut.

He stared dully out the rain-streaked window while the taxi glided over the dark wet streets. He thought about Mr. Barnaby and *The Magical Night*. Had he read the last chapter? Would he still publish the book, now that Adrienna had died? Mr. Barnaby was his last link to his mother and he desperately needed to talk to him.

The taxi dropped them in front of Will's building. He had a sudden terrifying vision of being dumped in a foster home. He'd stayed with Mrs. Ginny for the past week. She'd been so kind, not forcing him to talk about his mother like the social worker who'd come to visit, but he was sure she wouldn't want a kid around all the time.

"You're an orphan now," said Aunt Mauve. "The social worker and I discussed the situation. You belong to me. You and your mon…"

Aunt Mauve snapped her mouth shut.

"What?" said Will. "Me and my what?"

But Aunt Mauve had sealed her lips.

An orphan! Will had read lots of books with orphans in them, but he didn't think that was a word people still used in real life.

"You can wash dishes and scrub floors," said Aunt Mauve.

She ordered Will to pack his trunk. He put in his most prized possessions first – his stack of writing books filled with the beginnings to his novels, his mother's empty pencil box, a thesaurus full of amazing words and a brand-new writing book with an emerald cover. His mother had bought it for him at *Abracadabra*, and he had been saving it.

He opened the thesaurus and looked up the word *orphan*. He read the words that followed: *foundling, urchin, gamin, waif, stray*. They jumped around like ping-pong balls in his stomach.

That night, with an aching heart, he moved into Aunt Mauve's cramped dark house on the other side of the city.

chapter two

AUNT MAUVE

)

"THERE'LL BE NO WRITING in this house!" said Aunt Mauve. She stood in the doorway of Will's tiny bedroom, her eyes flashing.

Will stared at the top of the dresser where he had stacked his writing books and the royal blue pencil box. The books were gone. His stomach lurched. "My novels!" he cried.

"You're too late," crowed Aunt Mauve. "I tossed them in the rubbish while you were at school."

Will shoved his way past Aunt Mauve and raced down the narrow hallway and through the kitchen. He yanked the lid off the trash bin that stood on the back step and stared, horrified, at a lone banana peel.

"No use looking in there!" screeched Aunt Mauve. "The trash was picked up at noon. Your books are gone. Every last one."

She disappeared into the living room and turned on the TV. Will stormed back to his bedroom and flung himself on the bed. He felt sick at the thought of losing all those words. "Witch!" he muttered under his breath.

He rolled onto his side and studied the pencil box. At least Aunt Mauve hadn't thrown that away. Suddenly, a pale golden light seeped out from under the lid of the box, as if there were a tiny sun trapped inside. His mouth dropped open. He sat up and reached for the box. Holding his breath, he opened the lid. The light had disappeared. There was nothing inside.

It was crazy! There *had* been a light, but now it had vanished. The box came from the *Abracadabra* shop. Was it a magic box? Even the possibility sent a chill through him.

He closed the lid, waited and then opened it one more time. Nothing.

For a second, he thought about telling Aunt Mauve about the box, but she would accuse him of lying. Mr. Barnaby would be interested, but Will didn't know if he would ever see Mr. Barnaby again.

After a long time, he knelt on the floor and reached into his trunk. He took out the brand-new writing book. He sat on the bed and opened the cover. A clean lined page stared back at him. He waited for the usual thrill of excitement, but instead he felt afraid. He hugged his cold arms. When his mother had died, something died inside Will too.

"I can't write any more," he whispered. "I just can't!"

❖

It took Will two hours and four bus transfers to get all the way across the city to his school. One afternoon, when school was finished, he walked the eight blocks to the brick building where he had lived all his life. He lingered on the street, shivering in his thin jacket, and watched lights blink on in their old window. A small boy's face appeared, pressed against the glass. He waved.

Then someone pushed him away and pulled the curtains, shutting out the empty street and Will.

Something tingled inside Will. The plot for a new novel? What if the boy was one of those kids you heard about on the news who had been abducted? He'd make the kidnapper an insane wizard who... A sickening feeling of despair welled up in him again. He heard a clanking sound and spun around. The knight in shiny armour and the woman with the wreath were standing beside a lamppost.

"Leave me alone!" shouted Will. "I don't write any more!"

He ran, away from the Muses and away from his old flat, all the way to the office of Barnaby Book Publishers Inc. He banged hard on the narrow black door, but no one came. He peered through the post slot. Piles of letters were scattered across the floor, but not the large brown envelope containing Adrienna's last chapter. It looked like Mr. Barnaby had gone away. He had deserted Will.

Will waited a long time for a bus and it was dark before he got back to Aunt Mauve's house. He carried his cold supper of fried eggs into the living room, where his aunt sat glued in front of the television. He had given up looking through the TV Guide, because they always watched Aunt Mauve's favourite game shows. Aunt Mauve was supposed to be looking for a job, but in the three weeks that he had lived in her house, she had only ventured out once, to buy their meagre groceries.

The next day, two things arrived in the post that changed his life forever.

chapter three

MAGIC!

))

HUNCHED OVER HIS GREASY SAUSAGES, Will heard the doorbell ring. Aunt Mauve stopped slurping her cup of tea and said, "That'll be the postman."

"Maybe it's a job offer," said Will. He'd given up on Mr. Barnaby and his talk about money, and he was worried that soon there would be nothing to eat in the house. He raced to the door.

Aunt Mauve got there first. "Don't give me any of your sass!" she cried. She scooped up a long white envelope lying on the carpet and stuffed it in the pocket of her dressing gown. She disappeared into her bedroom. Will abandoned the sausages and got his backpack.

"I'm leaving for school," he called from the dingy hallway. He opened the door and almost stepped on a package wrapped in brown paper that the postman had left on the step. The words Master William Poppy leapt out at him. He picked up the package and tucked it into his backpack.

Aunt Mauve appeared suddenly in her purple boots and squirrel cape. The top of the white envelope peeked out of her big black purse.

"Where are you going?" asked Will.

"Places. Not that it's any of your business."

Something's happened, thought Will. He twisted his head to see the envelope. In the corner there was a very large colourful stamp with a kangaroo on it and the word Australia. Who would write a letter to Aunt Mauve from Australia? He followed his aunt up the road to the bus stop, sloshing around puddles.

Will's bus arrived first. He sat on the back seat, squeezed between two men with drippy umbrellas. He twisted around, keeping his aunt in sight through the foggy window until the bus rumbled around the corner.

What was Aunt Mauve up to? What was in that big white envelope?

�֍

The two men got off three stops later and Will had the seat to himself. He took the package out of his backpack and tore off the brown wrapping. Inside was something hard wrapped in tissue paper with a note taped to the top. The note said,

> Will, dear,
> The new tenant in your flat found this at the back of a cupboard. I meant to send it to you weeks ago. I hope this finds you, if not happy, at least well.
> Your friend, Mrs. Ginny.

He pulled back the tissue paper and unwrapped a photograph in a gold frame. It was a picture of a man, a woman and a little girl, sitting on a blanket under a tree beside a picnic basket. At first, he thought the woman was his mother. He turned the frame over. On the back someone had written Adrienna, Carmelita and Sterling. Adrienna's sixth birthday.

The little girl was his mother, and the man and the woman were his grandparents! He had never seen a picture of them before. He studied their faces. His grandfather, Sterling, had a determined square chin and haunting black eyes. Carmelita had been a dancer and was very glamorous. She had died the Christmas after Adrienna turned eight, and Sterling had left Adrienna in the care of a housekeeper.

"Your grandfather passed away the year before you were born," Adrienna had said once. "You have my blue eyes and brown hair, but you have your grandfather's chin. He was a writer like you."

Will started to wrap the photograph back in the tissue paper when he spotted a piece of cloth, rolled up tightly and buried in the rustling paper. He unrolled a long narrow strip of woven material. It had jagged edges as if it had been cut roughly out of a larger piece. Silver stars glittered against a royal blue sky. Woven into the design in gold thread as delicate as spiderwebs were the words:

The Griffin of Darkwood

The Griffin of Darkwood? What did it mean? A griffin was Will's favourite mythological creature. He'd seen a painting of one in a library book. He'd been in awe of its powerful lion's body, outstretched wings and magnificent eagle's head with snow-white feathers, curved beak and piercing eyes.

Where had the scrap of cloth come from? One word popped into Will's head – Magic!

The bus driver announced his stop. Hastily he rolled

up the cloth, wrapped it and the photograph in the brown paper, put the package in his backpack and scrambled off the bus.

�֍

When Will got back to Aunt Mauve's house that evening, it was empty. He shut his bedroom door, unzipped his backpack and took out the photograph of Adrienna and his grandparents. He lay on his bed and stared at it. Then he unrolled the cloth and examined it.

The magical feeling on the bus had disappeared. The cloth had probably slipped into the tissue paper by mistake. It might be a piece of an old tablecloth or part of a curtain belonging to Mrs. Ginny. He rolled it up again and put it in the pencil box, with the photograph on top. The pencil box was acting very ordinary now, but Will knew he hadn't imagined the mysterious light.

At ten o'clock, the front door rattled. Aunt Mauve had forgotten her key. Will opened the door with a huge yawn. "I'm going to be dead for school tomorrow. I was fast asleep."

"You're not going to school tomorrow," said Aunt Mauve.

"What?"

"You have to pack. We're moving to a place in the country. That's why I'm so late. I was making arrangements all day and missed the last bus."

"Moving? No way!" said Will. "Forget it! I've got friends at school! Besides, how can you afford a house in the country?"

"It's not just a house. I've bought an estate! It's called Sparrowhawk Hall."

For a second, Aunt Mauve shrank under Will's astounded stare. "Well...not quite what I intended...it was extraordinary...it was like I was under some kind of spell."

"A spell!" said Will. "What do you mean?"

"The agent was a very peculiar man. I told him I was looking for a cottage in a little village outside of London. He didn't seem to hear a word I said. He made me feel quite dizzy. It was his eyes. Before I knew it, I was signing the deeds to Sparrowhawk Hall."

"You're crazy," said Will. "You should go back and tell him you've changed your mind."

"I tried," said Aunt Mauve. "After I got a few blocks away, my head cleared, and I went right back. But the office had disappeared."

"That's impossible," said Will.

Aunt Mauve glared at him. "Anyway, the idea is growing on me." She took a piece of paper out of her black purse. She read out loud. "Sparrowhawk Hall. Elegant country estate in quaint village. Includes two loyal servants."

"An elegant country estate! Two loyal servants! That would cost a fortune!"

"It was cheap, for your information. A bargain."

"Because no one else wanted it!" said Will.

"I'll take none of your lip," said Aunt Mauve. "You miserable child, you can start packing."

chapter four

SPARROWHAWK HALL

)

THE MOVERS PICKED UP the packing boxes and Will's trunk at the end of the week. The next morning, Will and Aunt Mauve took a taxi to the bus station. Will stared out the taxi window at the city streets, his stomach clenched. Leaving London made him feel like he was losing his mother forever.

The bus was almost full. Will shoved his backpack and his aunt's big battered suitcase into the overhead rack. His aunt pushed ahead of him and took the window seat.

She was wearing her squirrel cape. Will breathed through his mouth so he didn't have to smell the mothballs, and he tried to ignore the row of glassy eyes and look out the window, but he soon gave up.

The bus was stuffy and warm and his eyes refused to stay open. The next thing he knew, it was dark outside and the lights in the bus had dimmed. The bus driver called out, "Last stop. End of the line."

Will dragged Aunt Mauve's suitcase and his backpack down from the rack and followed his aunt off the bus. A cold wind blew and thunder rumbled.

"Over there!" Will had spotted another bus at the far end of the station. Its lights were on and a sign in the front window said *Sparrowhawk*.

The bus was much smaller than the first, and the driver was a gaunt man wearing a wool knit cap and a plaid jacket. "Tickets," he muttered.

Aunt Mauve couldn't find the tickets. While she hunted through her bulging handbag, only one other passenger boarded. It was a woman with frizzy hair wearing a long red skirt and strings of beads. "Evening, Purvis," she said.

The driver grunted.

The woman smiled at Will and passed to the back of the bus.

"Here they are!" Aunt Mauve produced the two tickets and plunked herself down in a seat a few rows back. Will sat in the first seat, so he could see out the front window.

The door swung shut and the bus pulled out of the station. Its headlights lit up a narrow strip of black road with blowing trees on either side. The road climbed, gradually at first and then with steep switchbacks. *We've gone right over the top of a mountain!* thought Will, as they began a sharp descent that made his stomach do a flip.

What if? he thought suddenly. *What if the bus was really a giant rollercoaster and the driver was an evil gnome? What if he'd tampered with the tracks?*

Something made Will spin around. The Muses were back, sitting in the rear of the bus on either side of the woman who was reading. "Why didn't they listen the first time?" he muttered. "Why are they here? I don't want them! I don't write any more!"

Will shut his eyes tight and then opened them, and the Muses were gone. He stared out the window. After a while, he lost count of how many times the bus climbed and descended, rattling and swaying around corners.

"You're the ones who bought Sparrowhawk Hall," said the driver.

A fork of lightning streaked across the black sky. Will saw a river and a jumble of village roofs and then the bus plunged back into darkness. Thunder crashed.

The driver grunted. "Stirrin' things up. No business being here. Go back where you came from!"

Another jagged fork of lightning lit up the sky. "For heaven's sake, Purvis Sneed!" said a voice behind Will.

He twisted around in his seat. The woman with the frizzy hair was standing in the aisle. "Pay no attention to Purvis, or for that matter, to any of the others."

Will stared at the woman. What did she mean, the others?

"We've had enough death –" Purvis began. His next words were drowned in a peal of thunder but Will heard him say, "You'll be sorry. You'll wish you'd never heard of Sparrowhawk Hall!"

The bus swerved around a sharp corner, over a stone bridge and under an old brick archway. With a rattle and a jerk, it came to a stop. Purvis turned off the bus lights and swung open the door. Will lugged Aunt Mauve's suitcase and his backpack off the bus. They were parked at the end of a cobblestone square. Narrow streets dimly lit with old-fashioned lamps disappeared in every direction between the dark buildings. The storm stopped as suddenly as it had begun, and through a break in the clouds, a full moon beamed down.

The woman gestured toward a street that rose steeply from the square. "Stay on Black Penny Road. It'll take you right through the village and up to Sparrowhawk Hall."

A large Persian cat rubbed up against the woman's leg. It had rich gold fur with black around its eyes. "Here's Macavity come to meet me," she said.

She disappeared up one of the twisting streets with Macavity following close behind. Purvis Sneed vanished up an alley. Pale moonlight bathed the square. A hand-painted sign that read EX LIBRIS hung over a nearby doorway, creaking as it swung back and forth in the wind.

"I think it's a book shop," said Will. He pressed his face against the window. A lamp cast enough light for him to make out shelves crammed to the ceiling with books and more books piled up on the floor. A tiny figure, with big pointed ears, sat cross-legged on the floor, hunched over an open book.

"Someone's in there!" said Will.

"Books! Is that all you think about?" snapped Aunt Mauve. "Perhaps your highness could pick up my suitcase and we could get going!"

Reluctantly, Will pulled himself away from the window, and he and Aunt Mauve started walking up Black Penny Road. The street was narrow and steep with twists and turns. The lamps cast odd shadows. They passed other streets with strange names – Three Cats Lane, Half Moon Road, Goatsbeard Road, Shadow Alley.

Shop signs hung over dark doorways. They passed a bakery, a hardware shop, a delicatessen, a chemist's, a dress shop and a shoe shop. Above the shops were windows with tightly closed wooden shutters. Light peeped through the cracks, and in the occasional window without shutters, curtains twitched as they walked by. The suitcase was heavy and Will had to switch arms several times.

Black Penny Road passed under another archway of

crumbling brick. From there the road climbed until they looked down on the grey moonlit roofs of the village. They passed a scattering of little stone houses and rounded the final bend in the road.

"Aunt Mauve!" gasped Will. "You've bought a castle!"

"Don't be ridiculous," said Aunt Mauve. "I detest castles!"

They were indeed staring at an ancient stone castle. The enormous walls were like blank grey faces with narrow windows for eyes. At one end a round tower rose high above the castle roof. At the other end loomed a massive square tower, half in ruins. A pink van was parked in the weeds that grew right up to the castle walls.

A sign nailed to a huge oak tree announced in bold letters: SOLD.

"Come on!" shouted Will.

They waded through the weeds to the front of the castle. A granite gargoyle crouched on its haunches on top of an archway. It had a dog-like face with sunken eyes, flaring nostrils and big ears.

On the other side of the archway, a heavy wooden door creaked opened. A tall thin man in a black suit and a short thin woman in a black dress stepped out of the shadows.

"They must be the loyal servants," whispered Will.

chapter five

THE TOWER

☾

"WE'VE BEEN WAITING for you," said the woman. "A trunk and some boxes were delivered yesterday. My name is Mrs. Cherry and I am the housekeeper. This is Mr. Cherry. He will be your butler."

Mrs. Cherry had pursed purple lips and tightly permed brown hair. Will couldn't stop staring at a single black hair that sprang out of a mole on her chin. Mr. Cherry's hair was black and oily and he had a long pointed nose. His skin was sallow with a greyish tinge. His white wrists and hands dangled out of the ends of his jacket sleeves.

"I also do the cooking," Mrs. Cherry continued.

"I like everything fried," said Aunt Mauve. "And I never eat breakfast before eleven o'clock and –"

"Really," said Mrs. Cherry. "We were hired two weeks ago by the Linley estate to put things in order. You understand there is a lot to do. Now, if Madame would care to come inside."

Aunt Mauve and Will walked between the servants into a large entrance hall. The room was like ice. The walls were stone and the high stone ceiling was supported by wooden timbers. A dusty suit of armour glinted dully in the corner and two crossed swords hung on the wall above a yawning fireplace. At one end of the entrance hall rose a wide stone staircase. At the other end was a low curved wooden door half-hidden in a shadowy alcove. All along the walls narrow passageways disappeared into darkness.

"This is the part of the castle where the living quarters are," said Mrs. Cherry. "The castle was built by a king but the Linley family have owned it for generations. There are seventy-three rooms. The last Linleys who lived here put in water pipes and electricity. Otherwise it has been quite unchanged for centuries."

She glanced at Mr. Cherry. "We've been paid to stay for another month. I'm quite sure our work will be finished by then."

"We've put you, Madame, in the Red Chamber in the west wing," said Mr. Cherry in a high-pitched voice. "We've put the brat...uh, the boy, in the round tower."

"I'll show you to your room," said Mrs. Cherry, walking right past Aunt Mauve's suitcase.

Aunt Mauve scowled, picked up her suitcase and followed Mrs. Cherry down one of the narrow passageways. Will was alone with Mr. Cherry.

The man took a huge ring of keys from his pocket. He inserted an old-fashioned key in a brass lock in the low curved wooden door and swung the door open. Will peered past him at a stone spiral staircase. Mr. Cherry leaned over until his long pointed nose almost touched Will's forehead. The nauseating smell of garlic wafted over Will. He wanted to jump back, but he forced himself to keep still. Mr. Cherry shoved him onto the first step. "Find your own way from here!" He slammed the door shut.

Will shivered but it wasn't with fright. His whole life he had wanted to sleep in a tower.

✣

The steps twisted around and around and were very narrow and steep. Lamps set in small alcoves lit the way. Centuries of footsteps had worn smooth hollows in the stone. At the top of the winding staircase, Will stepped under a low arch into a small round room lit by a brass lamp on the wall.

The heads of birds circled the room above his head, carved into the round stone walls about a foot below the ceiling. They glared down at him, each one with sharp eyes and a curved beak like a bird of prey. Were they sparrowhawks?

Set into the walls were four deep narrow windows, open to the air with wooden shutters on either side. There was very little furniture – an old four-poster bed and a little round table and chair. His trunk was on the floor at the end of the bed.

He spotted a wooden trap door in the ceiling above the bed. He scrambled onto the bed and reached his hands up and pushed against the door. It lifted and fell backwards, and he pulled himself up and out, onto the roof of the tower.

Ke-ke-ke-ke. Two birds, perched on top of the parapet, flapped away into the night. The moonlight made everything almost as bright as day. Will could see the entire castle. It was built around a courtyard, filled with rubble and overgrown with weeds. At least half of the castle was in ruins.

He had read every book in the school library about

medieval castles. He stared at the huge square tower at the opposite end of the courtyard. "That's the keep," he murmured.

Part of the keep had broken away, leaving a gaping black hole and heaps of smashed stone on the ground below. The entrance was buried. He knew from reading his books that inside the keep was a huge room called the great hall. He would love to see a real great hall, but it would take a bulldozer to get inside there.

Will tilted his head back and felt the wind on his face. And then, in the wind, he heard his mother's soft voice.

"Towers and magic," whispered Adrienna Poppy. "Anything can happen in a castle like this, William Poppy. Anything."

chapter six

TAP TAP TAP!

☽

WILL CRAWLED UNDER the thin blanket on the bed. The moonlight made strange shadows on the stone walls. The carved birds seemed alive, watching him, wondering why he was in their tower. He felt the beginning of a story spinning in his head.

Suspicious, Will climbed out of bed and ran to a window. The Muses were standing in the long grass, the knight's shiny armour glowing in the moonlight.

"LEAVE ME ALONE!" shouted Will. He was never going to write again. Never! He wanted nothing to do with the Muses. He climbed back into bed and, after a long time, fell asleep.

He woke up with freezing toes and fingers. Bits of a strange dream scrambled about in his head. *I was in this tower*, he thought. *I was in this bed. Someone was in the room with me, holding a candle. Someone said, "The child is very ill."*

The dream had switched suddenly, like dreams do. He had heard the word *traitor* and boots pounding down the spiral stairs. He remembered staring at a dark pool in the middle of the stone floor. Blood! And then he had wakened.

Suddenly, a golden light shone from Adrienna's pencil box on the little round table. *Magic! Again!* With his eyes fixed on the box, Will slid out of bed. But as he opened the box, the light faded away, and there was nothing inside except his grandparents' photograph and the rolled-up cloth.

Will peeked through one of the deep windows. Low-lying fog hid the village and surrounding valleys. He dressed in his jeans and wool socks and set out to explore the castle. He scrambled down the tower stairs to the entrance hall with the swords and the suit of armour. From there he ventured through a maze of narrow stone passageways and up and down staircases. An occasional dim light bulb lit his way.

The castle was as cold as a tomb. The rooms were furnished with huge tables, stiff couches, cumbersome dressers and tall dark wardrobes. Portraits of gloomy-faced men and women in gilt frames glowered down from the walls. Heavy velvet curtains hung over the windows and fireplaces yawned like empty black mouths.

He peered through a doorway. The room beyond had crimson velvet curtains and a great canopy of crimson satiny cloth that hung over a high four-poster bed. The Red Chamber! Aunt Mauve's suitcase lay open in the middle of the bed, spilling out stockings and scarves, but there was no sign of Aunt Mauve.

Will headed down a dark sloping passageway that felt like it led to the very back of the castle. A man with a round red face, dressed in a white coat and tall white chef's hat, bustled past him.

"Hello," said Will. He was sure Mrs. Cherry had said she did all the cooking.

The man didn't answer. He muttered, "A brace of pheasants. We need a brace of pheasants."

Will opened a door at the end of the passageway and stared in surprise.

It was the kitchen and it was deliciously warm. Crackling logs blazed in a huge stone fireplace. Mrs. Cherry rested in an armchair beside the hearth, her feet propped up on a footstool and a cup of tea beside her.

"What do you want?" she asked.

"Nothing." Will spotted a huge stone sink and an ancient-looking stove, but he couldn't see anything to eat.

"It's a big castle for my husband and me to look after," said Mrs. Cherry. "No one should begrudge me a few minutes of rest."

"I don't," said Will.

Mrs. Cherry slurped her tea. "I suppose your aunt will be demanding breakfast."

"I don't know where she is."

Mrs. Cherry closed her eyes.

"Are we having pheasant for dinner?" said Will.

"In your dreams," said Mrs. Cherry. "Fish pie if you're lucky."

"Yuck," said Will. He headed back along the sloping passageway.

Tap, tap, tap!

He stopped beside a heavy wooden door that was ajar and looked into a long narrow room. In the middle was the biggest dining-room table he had ever seen. At the far end of the room, Mr. Cherry was kneeling beside an enormous fireplace, tapping a hammer against a wall of dark wood paneling.

"What are you doing?" asked Will.

Mr. Cherry dropped the hammer. He whirled around and stood up. His eyes blazed. "How DARE you sneak up on me!"

"I didn't! I was just looking around." Will stared at the wall. "Is there something wrong?"

Mr. Cherry picked up the hammer and edged toward him. "Dry rot," he muttered. "Are you interested in castles?"

"Yes, I am."

"Follow me."

Mr. Cherry led Will along dim passageways and up long flights of dark stairs. *We must be going to the very top of the castle,* Will thought. He glanced into some of the rooms as they went past. They were empty, the floors covered in a thick layer of dust. The back of his neck prickled. Was Mr. Cherry trying to get him alone? No one would ever hear him if he yelled for help.

Then Will said, "Wait a minute. What was that? It sounds like someone crying."

"I don't hear anything," said Mr. Cherry. "That's the trouble with boys. They have foul imaginations!"

Will checked back over his shoulder as he followed Mr. Cherry, but he saw no one.

"This is it," Mr. Cherry said finally. "The guard's walk."

They were at one end of a long narrow corridor with peepholes in the thick stone wall. Will stood on tiptoe and peered through one of the openings. All he could see was grey sky.

"We're very high up," said Mr. Cherry. "You'll have to come out here if you want to see the view."

He opened a low door and had to stoop to go through. Will followed him onto a narrow balcony with a stone wall.

"Take a look," snarled Mr. Cherry.

Will leaned over the wall. His stomach dropped. This side of the castle rose straight up from a high craggy cliff, almost as if it were growing right out of the rocks. Far, far below was the black river. Two sleek birds circled above the water. *We're even higher than the birds*, thought Will. It made his head spin.

"It's a long way down," Mr. Cherry whispered close to his face. Garlicky fumes made Will feel sick.

"People would say 'Such a terrible accident,'" Mr. Cherry breathed in his ear.

Will felt Mr. Cherry's hand press between his shoulder blades. He gasped. The man was crazy! He yanked himself away, his heart pounding. He ducked through the door back into the hallway. *Run!* A voice screamed in his head. *Run! Run!*

Will's feet pounded the stone floor. He whipped around corners. Behind him echoed Mr. Cherry's maniacal laughter.

And then it was silent. Will slid into a doorway, sucking in gulps of air. He heard footsteps and Mr. Cherry strode by him, only an arm's-length away. Will sagged against the wall, his legs like porridge.

chapter seven

EX LIBRIS

)

WILL STOOD OUTSIDE the archway at the front of the castle. He glanced up at the creepy stone gargoyle. Then he noticed something on the huge wooden door. Someone had sprayed the words GO AWAY in red paint.

"Go back to where you came from," the bus driver had said. And the woman on the bus had said, "Don't pay any attention to the others." The glaring words on the door made him feel sick. Why were people so scared of him and his aunt? What had Purvis Sneed meant when he said there was too much death?

Will set out down the steep Black Penny Road to the village. The fog had lifted but it was a damp morning. A woman standing on the doorstep of the first stone house stared at him, unsmiling. As he continued down the road, he felt the woman's eyes on his back.

People were out with their shopping bags in the square. They watched Will as he walked past. He went straight to the bookstore. When he opened the door, a bell under the EX LIBRIS sign jingled. With a yelp, a girl crashed into him and dropped a book. She was dressed all in black, with red hair that fell to her waist and big round glasses.

"Sorry," said Will. He picked up the book and handed it to her. Without a sound, she scurried past him.

He went inside. Bookshelves reached right to the ceiling in every direction, so it was impossible to tell if it was a big shop or a small shop. There was an old-fashioned rolltop desk at the front, but nobody was there.

"Hey!" he called.

"Back here," a voice said.

There were several ways Will could go. He eased between two towering bookshelves, turning sideways to squeeze past the places where books stuck out. The narrow aisle veered right and then left and then came to a dead end.

Wrong way, he thought, turning around and sliding between the books until he was back at the rolltop desk. He chose the second route, which ended at a saggy armchair, leaking stuffing, with books scattered around it on the floor.

The third route looked more promising; the books were tidier and not sticking out so much. After a few sharp turns he emerged into a small clearing somewhere in the middle of the shop. A man stood by a table, writing something on a sheet of cardboard. He was the tallest man Will had ever seen, with a long face like a horse and grey hair tied back in a neat ponytail.

"You made it!" he said. He smiled. "You must be the boy from the castle."

"Right," said Will.

The man stuck out his hand. "I'm Favian Longstaff. Welcome to Sparrowhawk."

"I'm Will Poppy." They shook hands.

"Did you see Madeleine de Luca?" said Favian. "She

was just leaving."

"She was in an awful hurry." Will gazed around. "You could get lost in this shop!"

"Oh, yes," said Favian. "A man did once. He was lost for weeks. He came in clean-shaven and went out with a beard!" He grinned. "Just kidding! Now, how do you like the castle?"

"Very cool," said Will. "Except for the servants who look after the place. They are seriously awful."

"I've had a few unpleasant encounters with them," said Favian. "How is Mrs. Cherry's cooking?"

"What cooking? There was nothing for breakfast. But I'm still hoping for pheasant for supper. It sounds more interesting than fish pie."

Will told Favian about the chef he had seen in the passageway to the kitchen.

"Ah, you've met Cookie!"

"He acted like he didn't see me."

"I don't suppose he did." Favian's eyes twinkled. "He's one of Sparrowhawk Hall's resident ghosts!"

"A ghost! Yeah, right. You're kidding again."

"Scout's honour. He was the castle's cook in the eighteenth century. The Lord Linley who owned the castle at that time was a difficult man to please. Cookie is always worrying about something. Often he's hunting for his rolling pin!"

Will let this sink in. A haunted castle. "Are there any more ghosts?"

"Oh, yes. There's a boy who can be heard sobbing. No one's ever spotted him, but he cries like his heart is breaking. You're not afraid, are you?"

"Who me? No way. I heard the boy! It was at the top

of the castle. Mr. Cherry took me there to see the guard's walk."

For a second, he wondered if he should tell Favian that Mr. Cherry had almost pushed him over. It would sound crazy, like he was paranoid. Favian would think he was a total nutcase.

"Any chance you're sleeping in the tower?" asked Favian.

"Yeah," said Will. "It's pretty awesome."

"I had a friend called Hannah Linley. She slept in the tower too. It had been sealed for hundreds of years and Hannah's father reopened it when he put electricity in the castle."

"Why was it sealed?"

"I don't know. The story is that there was a murder in the tower. Perhaps the tower was sealed then."

"I had a dream about blood! Who was murdered?"

"Nobody knows. It was so long ago. It might have been a Linley. Linleys have always owned the castle. Blood! Some things are best left in the past. And now, young man, what can I do for you?"

"Fantasy," said Will.

"You've come to the right place! Fantasy is the only thing you'll find in here."

A fantasy bookstore! Will couldn't believe his luck.

"You can read right here in the shop. If you can't afford to buy a book, I'll lend you as many as you can carry."

Will looked at the cardboard on the table. It was a poster that said:

COME TO A READING
AT EX LIBRIS
RENOWNED POET VESPERA MOONSTONE
WILL READ HER POEMS
7:00 P.M. MAY 9

"Is she, like, a real poet?' he asked. "Has her stuff been published?"

"Absolutely."

"Is everyone invited?"

"Of course," said Favian.

"Even me?"

Favian looked at him quizzically. "Why not?"

"People haven't been exactly friendly." Will told Favian about the words GO AWAY sprayed on the door.

Favian frowned. "Unacceptable. But never mind." He wrote *Everyone Welcome* on the bottom of the poster. "That means you too."

Then he led the way to the front of the shop. He settled down to read at the rolltop desk, while Will drifted up and down the aisles, choosing books. He had accumulated a fair-sized pile when the bell over the front door jingled.

"I've come for my book," said a familiar high-pitched voice.

Mr. Cherry! What would he want in a fantasy bookstore? Will watched him from behind a tower of books.

Favian pulled down the lid of the rolltop desk, and loose papers and pens and paper clips showered everywhere. "Not here," he said cheerfully. "I know I ordered it. Now where the dickens did I put it?"

He rummaged through stacks of books on the floor,

while Mr. Cherry scowled and tapped his foot. Then Favian turned to a wobbly wall of books and beamed. "Aha!" he shouted.

He grabbed a book from near the top, and the wall tipped and tilted and crashed to the floor. A fat six-hundred-page volume called *An Encyclopedia of Little People* landed on Mr. Cherry's foot, and Mr. Cherry exploded with a very nasty word.

"Here it is." Favian held up a book with a picture of a castle on the shiny cover. *"Medieval Castle Construction and Design.* I think you'll find it –"

"It's not for me, it's for my nephew," growled Mr. Cherry. He grabbed the book, threw some bills on the desk and left the shop, banging the door behind him.

A dog barked furiously, and Mr. Cherry cursed again. A girl's voice shouted, "No, Peaches! Down boy! DOWN!"

chapter eight

NEW FRIENDS

☽

WILL DROPPED HIS BOOKS on the desk. He and Favian dashed outside. A brown-and-white dog with floppy ears hung on to Mr. Cherry's pant leg.

"Get this beast off me!" he roared.

The dog growled and gripped harder. Mr. Cherry swung his castle book wildly in the air.

"Let go, Peaches!" a girl shouted. She was tall and slim with long fly-away brown hair. She grabbed the dog's collar and dragged him away.

Mr. Cherry's face was purple. "That dog's a menace! A monster! I'll shoot him next time I see him!"

He stormed off across the square.

"Peaches tries to bite that man every time he sees him," said the girl. "I can't stop him."

"It's not your fault," said Favian. "I want to bite him too! Emma, this is Will Poppy."

"Will Poppy! Everyone's talking about you," said Emma. "Do you think I could see inside the castle?"

"I guess so," said Will. He wasn't sure he was ready to make friends with anyone yet. He wanted to check things out in the village a bit longer.

"When?" demanded Emma.

Will sighed. *Persistent* would be a good word to describe her. "Let me get my books and we can go now."

They said good-bye to Favian and started the climb up Black Penny Road. "Are you going to read all those books?" asked Emma.

"Of course. I love reading."

"I don't. I'm glad you've come. It's been deader than ever around here. Most of the kids are away for the spring holidays. You've heard of Barnum and Bailey, right?"

"What?"

"Barnum and Bailey."

"Never heard of it."

"Never heard of it? Everyone's heard of Barnum and Bailey."

"Not me."

Emma stopped walking and stared at Will.

"Well, what is it?" said Will.

"It a circus. It's famous. They have shows all over the world! I'm going to be an acrobat in a circus when I'm older." She did a slick cartwheel on the cobblestones to demonstrate.

"The circus is my *passion*," she said. "Everyone should have a passion. What's yours?'

"Um ..." Before, Will would have said writing. That was how he thought of his life; Before and After. He shrugged.

"When I finally get out of Sparrowhawk, I'll be going to New York," said Emma.

"Let me guess," said Will. "Circus school."

A horn blared behind them. It was Mr. Cherry in the pink van. The road was so narrow that they had to press up against a building to let him pass. He glared at Peaches through the window and shook his fist. Peaches barked until the van disappeared around a corner.

"How old are you?" asked Emma.

"Twelve."

"School year?"

"Seven."

"Good! Same as me. Do people call you Willy?"

"Will," said Will firmly. He wanted to direct the attention away from him. "Why is your dog called Peaches?"

"He used to be called Jack. And then he stole ten peaches and ate every one!"

"*Ten?*" said Will.

"He grabbed them off the table when no one was looking. He had a stomach ache all night and moaned and groaned and now he won't touch a peach. He shakes when he sees one."

"Hey, Emma!" called a voice above them. Will looked up. A boy with a round face leaned out of a window above the street. "Come on up!"

"Just for a minute," said Emma. "We're going to the castle!" She opened a green door under a carved archway. Inside was a steep staircase. "This is my friend Thom Fairweather's place. Peaches, you can wait here."

Thom greeted them at the top of the stairs. He had a thatch of thick brown hair that stuck out in all directions as if it had been cut by six different barbers at the same time. There was a dusting of white on his nose and a blob of chocolate on his eyebrow.

"This is Will," said Emma. "He's in year seven like us and he's going to be living here."

"Hi," said Thom. "You better be quiet because Dad's asleep."

The flat was small and filled with a delicious baking smell. In one corner sprawled a huge jade tree in a ceramic pot; in the other corner was a large wooden loom strung with brightly coloured threads.

"I'll come to the castle too," said Thom. "I'm just putting the icing on my cake. Can you wait for me? I can't hurry this stage."

"I'm his official taster," said Emma as they followed Thom into the kitchen.

The kitchen counter was covered with egg shells, a bag of sugar tipped over, butter, baking chocolate, spoons dripping batter, mixing bowls and a whisk. A wobbly chocolate cake, two layers high, sat on a platter.

"Thom's learning to be a French chef," said Emma. "That's his passion. He's using his mother's old cookbook. It's called *Mastering the Art of French Cooking*, and it's by a famous person named Julia Child. Thom's going to be famous too." Emma turned to Thom. "Hey! Maybe you can come to New York too. Work at the Ritz or someplace."

Thom turned on an electric mixer. "I'm making meringue," he shouted over the roar. He lifted dollops of drippy white goo from his bowl with a spoon. "Do these look like stiff peaks to you?"

Emma seemed doubtful. She studied the huge cookbook lying open to a page smattered with chocolate. "Did you remember that the eggs had to be room temperature?"

There was a short silence.

"It also says to use –"

"I think they're stiff enough," said Thom tersely. "I'm supposed to dribble boiling syrup in this, but I don't have any. So this will have to do." He spread the runny meringue over the cake, which Will thought had sunk at least two inches in the last minute. Then he cut them each a slice.

He looked at Emma anxiously. "Well?"

"Delicious!" declared Emma, her mouth full of cake.

"It's called a French word." Thom spelled it out. *"Le Glorieux.* That's gotta mean a glorious cake."

It is a glorious cake, thought Will. *Sticky, sweet, gooey in the middle and very chocolatey.* "Scrumptious," he told Thom.

"I'll clean this up later," said Thom, looking pleased. "I just want to give Dad a piece. Then we can go to the castle."

"Thom's mum died when he was a baby and his dad can't walk and is in a wheelchair and he sleeps a lot because of headaches," Emma explained when Thom had gone.

Will thought about the long flight of stairs. "What does he do when he wants to go out?"

"Someone has to carry him down the stairs. Mum says he should move somewhere else, but he's lived here all his life."

"Come on," said Thom, who was back. "Let's go."

Peaches was lying on his tummy on the tile floor at the bottom of the stairs. He thumped his tail when he saw Thom, but he didn't get up. Thom stroked the dog's head. "What happened to Peaches? He's so upset."

"He ran into that horrible man from the castle," said Emma. "Peaches bit him on the leg, and Mr. Cherry tried to hit him with a book. Peaches despises him."

"Poor old buddy," said Thom.

"When Thom's near an animal, he feels the animal's

emotions," said Emma. "It's like a special power. It's because he's a Fairweather. It runs in his family."

"It doesn't happen to all Fairweathers," said Thom. "It doesn't happen to Dad."

"That must be very cool," said Will.

"Not always," said Thom. "When I volunteered at the animal shelter, I took on the feelings of all the sad dogs. I nearly passed out. It was more than I could stand. I had to leave."

Thom ruffled Peaches' ears and the dog sat up. "He's okay now," said Thom.

With Peaches at their heels, they climbed up Black Penny Road.

"So," said Emma, "do you think you're going to like living in a castle? Has anyone told you about the curse yet?"

"What curse?" asked Will. It was hard to keep up with Emma.

"A lot of old people say that a griffin put a curse on the castle," Thom explained. "Hundreds of years ago."

"A griffin!" gasped Will. He thought of the words on his scrap of cloth. *The Griffin of Darkwood.*

"Bad things have happened in this village," said Emma. "A girl died. My grandmother, Granny Storm, even knew her."

"She was related to my dad," said Thom. "She was his dad's cousin, I think."

Will felt cold. "The girl. Did she die in the round tower?"

Thom and Emma stared at him. "I don't know," said Emma. "Why?"

"That's where I'm sleeping. And I had this awful

dream. Someone kept saying 'The child is very ill.' I saw blood, too and I heard someone say 'Traitor!' Favian Longstaff had a friend called Hannah Linley who slept in the tower forty years ago. But he didn't say anything about her dying."

"There was a murder too," said Thom. "That's what all the old people say. No one knows who. It happened hundreds of years ago."

"And the castle's haunted," said Will. "I've already seen a ghost called Cookie, and I heard a boy crying!"

"Haunted!" said Thom. "Oh, man!"

They rounded the bend in the road and the ancient castle loomed before them. They stood still and stared at it.

"It was boarded up until two weeks ago," said Emma. "That's when those creepy servants came."

Ke-ke-ke-ke. They looked up at two birds circling the tower. "Sparrowhawks," said Thom.

"I thought so," said Will. "They were there last night."

Flap, flap, flap, glide. One of the sparrowhawks swooped down into the long grass and came back up with a limp body hanging in its mouth.

"It's caught a starling." Thom sounded shaky. "I know it's nature, but I never like to see it." He sighed. "Sometimes it's depressing being me."

"Let's go inside!" Emma burst out. "I want to see the tower first."

chapter nine

EXPLORING THE CASTLE

☽

WILL LED THE WAY into the castle.

"I really hate that thing," said Thom, gazing uneasily at the stone creature hovering above them. "What's it supposed to be, anyway?"

"I don't really know," said Will. "It gives me the creeps."

Emma and Thom were shocked at the words GO AWAY sprayed on the door.

"People hate us, and I don't get why," said Will.

"My granny says –" began Emma, and then she clamped her mouth shut.

"What?' demanded Will.

"Nothing."

They climbed up the steep spiral stairs to the tower and Will put his books on the round table.

"Sparrowhawks," said Thom, looking up at the row of glaring faces carved in stone. "There must be a hundred! How can you sleep with them staring at you?"

"I like them," said Will.

They peered out the deep narrow windows. Then they climbed through the trap door onto the roof, leaving Peaches in the middle of the bed. *"Hooo-wooo-hoo,"* he howled. A sparrowhawk swooped off the parapet with raucous cries and circled in the distance. *Ke-ke-ke.*

"Most of the castle is just a big ruin," said Thom. "Look at that big square tower. It's almost buried."

"That's the keep," said Will. "The great hall's in there, but you can't get in. The doors are behind all that rock."

"Hey, you can see my building!" said Thom.

"You can't see my house," said Emma. "It's hidden behind that church. It used to be an old apple barn."

Thom walked over to the other side. "You sure get a good view of the forest from up here. No one ever goes in there. Not even hunters."

"Why not?" asked Will.

"The curse," said Emma. "Everyone's afraid."

Will stared at the forest. Dark trees crowded together. *You wouldn't be able to see the sun in there,* he thought. A glimmer of an idea stirred inside him. *What if...*

No, no, NO! He had given up on writing. He spotted the Muses, standing between the trees at the edge of the forest. He glared at them and they faded away.

"Did you see anyone?" he asked Thom and Emma.

"No," they both answered.

Peaches barked. One by one, they lowered themselves back through the trap door and down onto the bed, where Peaches greeted them with rapturous licks. Thom and Will jumped to the floor and Emma somersaulted off.

"How is Peaches' training going?" asked Thom.

"Watch this!" said Emma.

She stood in front of her dog. Peaches braced his front feet and grinned.

"Sit!"

Peaches wagged his tail.

"I said SIT!"

Peaches flopped down on his side and stuck his shaggy paws in the air.

"STAY!"

Peaches sprang up and raced in a circle, barking. Then he leapt up and put his feet on Emma's chest. "Idiot!" she said.

They spent the next hour exploring the castle. On Emma's suggestion, they had a wild game of hide-and-seek, squeezing in and out of dusty nooks and crannies in the maze of rooms and passageways. Emma made up all the rules. You couldn't actually hide *inside* anything, like a cupboard or a wardrobe, and you had to give yourself up after ten minutes. They finally collapsed on an old velvet couch that gave off a puff of grey dust.

"Has anyone seen Peaches?" asked Emma.

No one had. The dog had vanished. Emma chewed her lip. "That could mean trouble. We better find him."

"Peaches! Peaches!" they hollered up and down the passageways.

Peaches bounded around a shadowy corner with a silky purple cloud trailing from his mouth.

"Aunt Mauve's nightgown," said Will, inspecting it.

Emma pounced. "Got it!" There was a ripping sound.

"*Hoo-whoo-hoo*," howled Peaches. And then his howl turned into a sharp bark. "*RUFF!*"

A figure suddenly appeared at the end of another dark passageway. Emma shrieked.

"Aunt Mauve!" said Will, staring. "Are you all right?"

Aunt Mauve's eyes were glazed and her lips were blue. She was wrapped up in a tattered pink bathrobe.

Emma stuffed the purple nightgown behind her back.

"These are my friends, Thom and Emma," said Will.

"I don't care if they're the King and Queen of Siam!" blazed Aunt Mauve. "I can't find my bedroom!"

A roller in her hair sprang loose and landed on Emma's sneaker. She screamed and flung it off. Aunt Mauve shot her an icy look. Then she glared at Will. "Stop gawking and tell me how to get back to the Red Chamber."

"You're in the wrong part of the castle." Will pointed down a narrow passageway. "You've got to go that way."

When she had gone, Emma said, "That was your *aunt?* She's a horror!"

"Forget about her," said Will. "Come on. I'm starving! Let's go to the kitchen and see if we can find something to eat."

"Is this where you saw that ghost?" asked Thom as they made their way down the back passageway.

"*Ooooo-oooo-ooooo,*" said Emma.

"Shut up," muttered Thom.

The kitchen was empty and the fire in the fireplace had died. Pots and pans were stacked untidily in the sink, and grease had congealed in a big black frying pan on the stove.

"I smell bacon and eggs," said Thom.

They opened and closed cupboard doors, finding only a few cans of vegetables and a sack of oatmeal.

Thom frowned. "I wonder where she keeps all her baking supplies."

"Trust me, she's not the baking type." Will rattled the door of a long tall cupboard. "Locked. That's where all the good stuff to eat is, I bet."

A door at the far end of the kitchen was partly open. Will peeked around it into a little sitting room with a shiny green couch, two shabby armchairs and an old TV.

"This must be where the Cherrys live," Will said over his shoulder.

"Don't go in," said Thom.

Will ignored him and took a step into the room. Behind the couch was another door, this one closed. He heard a murmur of voices. *That must be their bedroom,* he thought.

The book from the bookstore, *Castle Construction and Design,* lay on a small table. Will recognized it right away. There was a scrap of paper sticking out of it as if it marked a place. What was Mr. Cherry looking for?

The voices behind the door rose higher, but Will couldn't make out any words. He took a chance. He darted right into the room and flipped open the book to the marker. At the top of the page was a chapter heading that said *Secret Passages.* He scanned the first few sentences.

What medieval castle was complete without a secret passage? Some secret passages led to the exterior of the castle to allow the lord to slip out without his enemies knowing he had escaped. Others were used to bring supplies in and out during a siege or led to underground supplies of water –

"I told you!" shouted Mr. Cherry from behind the door. Will froze. "Purvis Sneed was there when they found the Linley girl. He heard her story."

Purvis Sneed, thought Will. *The bus driver!*

"It was forty years ago," said Mrs. Cherry. "How could he remember?"

"I need a few more days! I'll find a way in."

"It's getting too risky! That boy is snooping –"

"I'll get rid of the boy!" snarled Mr. Cherry.

"Just don't do anything stupid."

Heavy footsteps approached the door. Will turned and fled back into the kitchen. "We're outa here!" he hissed.

They sped up the sloping passageway, through the entrance hall and outside the castle. Raindrops splashed on the ground.

"What happened?" asked Thom.

"The Cherrys were in there. They were talking about Purvis Sneed and a girl. Mr. Cherry said she was a Linley. It might be the girl who died. Mr. Cherry said Purvis Sneed was there when they found her, whatever that means."

He told them about the book and the chapter titled *Secret Passages*. "He said he'll find a way in. I saw him tapping on a wall in the dining room with a hammer. He's gotta be looking for a secret passage. That's the only thing I can think of."

"Then we'll look too!" said Emma, her dark eyes sparkling.

"Now?" Thom looked alarmed.

"Why not?"

"I thought you were supposed to be working at your granny's shop today," said Thom.

Emma yelped. "You're right! And I'm late again! Dad is going to kill me! Please, please, *please* wait until tomorrow before you start looking."

Will looked at Thom.

"Be fair," wailed Emma. "It was my idea."

"Okay," said Will. It was hard to wait, but it would be way more fun with Emma.

"Let's meet at Thom's tomorrow morning," said Emma.

"Not too early," said Thom. "I'm making Cherry Tart Flambé tomorrow. You light it on fire. It's going to be mega-cool!" He turned to Will. "You could come to my place now, for lunch if you want."

"Sure!" Will was famished.

The rain pelted down as they raced along Black Penny Road, Peaches leaping puddles and barking wildly. Just before they rounded the bend, Will glanced back at the gloomy castle. He shuddered when he thought of Mr. Cherry's icy words.

I'll get rid of the boy.

chapter ten

LANTERN LANE

☽

THOM MADE PEANUT BUTTER and jelly sandwiches for lunch with slices of the glorious chocolate cake for dessert.

"I'm eating only pb and j sandwiches and French desserts for a whole year. I'm on my fifth month now," he said.

"Are you kidding me?" said Will. "Peanut butter and jelly? Couldn't you at least have picked something like pizza or cheese burgers?'

"It's an experiment to see if I can last. Anyway, I love peanut butter," said Thom. "It's very nutritious."

"Do you know how weird that sounds?"

"So? It's fast and it's cheap. Dad and I don't have a lot of money."

"And your dad lets you do this?"

"Yep. Dad took me to the doctor and he said it's fine with him as long as I have three carrots and a glass of milk every day."

"*Seriously* weird," said Will.

The afternoon flew by. Will and Thom used six decks of cards and built a huge castle. The best part was blowing on it and making it all tumble down.

Will got back to the Sparrowhawk Hall just in time for

supper. He sat alone at the long table in the dining room, reading one of his books, while Mr. Cherry brought in two plates of fish pie. By the time Aunt Mauve finally showed up, wearing her long black coat and squirrel cape, the pie was cold.

"Where were you?" said Will.

"If it's any of your business, I've been wandering around for an hour trying to find my way here."

Aunt Mauve's teeth chattered and Will said with a grin, "You should run everywhere like I do. It would keep you warm."

"Watch your mouth," said Aunt Mauve.

Will pushed his plate away. He was still full of pb and j sandwiches and chocolate cake. He picked up his book and stood up.

"Where are you going?" said Aunt Mauve.

"To my tower."

"I hope you're not doing anything bad up there." She squinted at Will. "I've a good mind to come up and see."

"You can't," said Will. "The stairs are too steep."

He left without saying good night to Aunt Mauve. When he got to his tower, he gazed around and thought, *This is mine!* He picked up his mother's pencil box. Aunt Mauve would never make it up here. She'd never touch his stuff again.

Tires crunched on the road below. Will put the box down and leaned out one of the narrow windows. Moonlight bathed the scene below. He watched the pink van disappear around the side of the castle. What was Mr. Cherry up to now? He ran to another window to see where the van had gone. It had stopped in front of an old shed beside a crumbling wall. Clouds drifted over the moon and everything went black. The van door slammed shut.

Suddenly, an outdoor light flooded the area around the shed. Mr. Cherry was standing at the back of the van. He opened the door and dragged out two long objects. Light glinted on metal. Will wasn't sure what they were but they looked heavy. Mr. Cherry disappeared with them inside the shed. On his way back to the van, he gazed up at the tower.

He sees me, thought Will. *He'll think I'm spying on him.* He ducked back inside and held his breath until he heard the van start up again. He peeked back out the window and saw red tail lights vanishing into the darkness.

✣

In the morning, Will went to the kitchen to tell Mrs. Cherry that he didn't want any breakfast. A woman with blonde hair was washing dishes in the stone sink, her back turned to him. Where had she come from? Was she another ghost? A radio was blaring loud music and Will shouted, "Tell Mrs. Cherry I'm not hungry."

He decided to go a different way back to his tower. At the end of a shadowy corridor, he spotted a wooden door, studded with pieces of black iron. It took a few hard tugs to open. Steep stairs cut into rough rock descended into darkness. He peered into the gloom, fascinated. Could this be the way to the dungeon? He ventured as far as the fourth step and stopped. It was too dark. He needed a torch.

Will was almost back at his tower door when he bumped into Mrs. Cherry, carrying a tray. "Take this to your aunt," she said. "I'm only doing a breakfast tray this once. I have a big castle to look after."

"You've got a helper," said Will, thinking of the strange blonde woman in the kitchen, but Mrs. Cherry just glared at him and handed him the tray.

Aunt Mauve was buried in a pile of blankets under the crimson canopy in the middle of the four-poster bed. "It's about time breakfast showed up," she snapped. She handed Will a list, written on a scrap of paper. "Take this into the village and don't dawdle!"

Will read the list:

3 hot water bottles
4 prs. wool socks
2 prs. wool mittens
1 wool scarf
1 box of gingersnaps

His heart sank. It would take forever to find all these things!

"How am I supposed to pay for this?" he grumbled.

"Tell them I'll be down later to set up an account," said Aunt Mauve. "In a pokey little village like this, they should say thank you very much for my business."

"Tell them yourself," said Will. He refused to go until Aunt Mauve dug in her purse and produced a few crisp bills. He frowned. How did she have money all of a sudden? He tried to peek to see if there was more, but his aunt snapped the purse shut.

Will raced to the tower to get his books to return to the bookstore and then clattered down the winding staircase. He wanted to check out one thing before he went to the village. He walked around the side of the castle to the old shed beside the crumbling stone wall. A shiny steel padlock hung from the door clasp. Will rattled the door but it was no use.

When he got back to the front of the castle, Mr. Cherry was standing in the tall weeds, staring at something.

"Come," he said. "You'll want to see this."

Will walked over slowly.

A sparrowhawk stood on top of a struggling pigeon. "He's stabbing it with his talons," said Mr. Cherry. "He'll do that until he kills it. Then he'll tear it apart and eat it." He grinned at Will. "I know. I've watched them before."

Horror filled Will. It would be a disaster if Thom saw this. He turned and ran all the way down the steep road into the village. It felt good to run, stretching his legs and sucking in gulps of air.

He spent the next hour wandering up and down the winding cobblestone streets. They disappeared under archways or ended at stone stairs to someone's curved doorway and he had to keep retracing his steps. He peered down the entrance to Shadow Alley. It was as gloomy as a dank cellar with tall dark buildings on either side.

A street called Lantern Lane was especially twisty. At the end was a tiny house with a small courtyard made of blue, red, purple and yellow tiles arranged like a rainbow. A lace curtain at the window moved and a big Persian cat gazed through the glass at Will.

It was Macavity, the cat who had met the woman at the bus. The cat squeezed his eyes shut and when he opened them again, they were a deep purple colour. Will watched the purple change to a brilliant emerald. He had never seen anything like it in his life. *Magic.*

Macavity jumped off the windowsill and disappeared.

Will wanted to have another look at the strange cat. He knocked on the door, but there was no answer. He left, winding his way back through the twists and turns of Lantern Lane, until he came out to the square.

He hurried across the square to the *Ex Libris* bookstore and went inside. Favian, who was scribbling on a piece of paper, glanced up at the jingle of the bell. "Morning, Will."

"Hey," said Will. "I've brought my books back."

He stared at the towering walls of books. This time there were four possible ways into the depths of the shop. "You've changed things."

"A bit of rearranging. An estate sale came in yesterday."

Will ventured in. He had picked out half a dozen books when he came across a wall of books only partially built, surrounded by untidy stacks of books. He reached for a book to add to the wall and turned around just in time to see a face peering at him. It had reddish skin, a short pointed beard and two horns sticking out of a mass of curly hair.

In a flash, it disappeared.

"Who's there?" said Will. He peered up and down and around some corners, searching for the owner of the face, and then made his way to the front of the shop.

"This is going to sound crazy," he said. "But I think I just saw Mr. Tumnus. You know, from *The Lion, The Witch and the Wardrobe*."

"Mr. Tumnus!" said Favian. "I've always felt that I wasn't alone in here!"

"And the night we came? I saw someone through the window. I think it might have been an elf."

"Indeed!"

Will watched Favian put a sign in the window advertising Vespera Moonstone's poetry reading. Beside it was a large colour photograph of Vespera Moonstone. She was the woman from the bus!

"Vespera Moonstone was on the same bus as Aunt Mauve and me. I didn't know she was the poet!" said Will. "She has this amazing cat."

"Macavity," said Favian. "Vespera Moonstone is our local celebrity. She just got back from a book tour in the United States."

"I just went to her house. I knocked, but she wasn't home."

"Vespera never answers the door when she's writing. She has an artistic temperament."

"My mother wrote a book. It's going to be published this year." Will hadn't known he was going to say that. The words just blurted out of him. And he wasn't even positive that it was still true.

"Really?" Favian looked so interested that Will told him all about his mother's book and Mr. Barnaby and Barnaby Book Publishers Inc. He shook when he told Favian that Adrienna had died.

"Oh, my," said Favian. "You *have* had a tough time. Your aunt sounds like a dragon. But you're living in a castle! That's one interesting thing. Your mother would approve of that."

"She'd love the castle!" said Will.

"So her book is called *The Magical Night*," said Favian. "Let's think positively. I'll order it for the shop and it will have a place of honour in the window. A mother who was a writer! How marvellous!"

"I used to be a writer too," said Will.

"I suspect that once a person is a writer, they're always a writer. I myself am a great reader, and once a reader, always a reader is what I say. The same must be true of writers, though I have no experience with it."

"I don't know." Will peeked at Favian's paper. "If you're not writing, what are you doing?"

"Palindromes." Favian's long dour face lit up. "They're a bit of an obsession with me."

"I've never heard of palindromes."

"They're words that are spelled the same way backwards or forwards. Like the word *racecar*." Favian printed it on the paper.

"That's so neat!" Will adored anything to do with words.

"I enter contests all the time. You can have phrases or whole sentences too. Here's one of my favourites."

With a chuckle, he wrote:

Murder for a jar of red rum

"I didn't make that one up myself, I'm sorry to say. Palindromes are a pastime that is thousands of years old. Some of the most powerful magic words in medieval times were palindromes."

He wrote on the paper: *odac dara arad cado*

"It's from an old medieval spell book. It means fly like a vulture."

The ancient words gave Will a thrill. It would be cool to think of palindromes too, like Favian. "I better go," he said. "I have to buy some stuff for my aunt and then I'm meeting my friends."

"Odac dara arad cado!" said Favian.

chapter eleven

MORGAN MOONSTONE

$$\smile)$$

IT TOOK AGES TO FIND the items on Aunt Mauve's list. The first shops Will went to had CLOSED signs hanging on their doors, and he was convinced that the shop owners had turned their signs around when they saw him coming. When a shop was open, no one helped him and he had to search the aisles by himself. At the end, he had some money left over so he looked for a torch.

"Don't carry torches," muttered the man in the hardware shop.

Will went back to the grocer and the woman said, "You again," and acted like she had never even heard of torches.

Finally, a man in a second-hand shop sold him a big silver torch. "You watch your step up there at the castle," he said.

Everyone knows who I am, Will thought. *It's spooky.*

Next door was a shop called *The Winking Cat*. He peered through the window and then went inside. A teenager with blond dreadlocks sat at a till listening to music. Sparkling rocks of all different colours were arranged on tables and piled in plastic boxes labelled with names like tiger's eye, sunstone, pink fire quartz, opals

59

and Apache tears.

"Crystals," said the boy at the till. He turned the music down. "They have powers. For divination and stuff like that. And they can protect you from things. I'm not really into it myself."

Long skinny candles, bunched together by their wicks, hung from the ceiling. One other customer, a girl with long red hair, was standing in front of a display of narrow boxes with a sign that said *Incense*. It was the girl from the bookstore. Will thought Favian had said her name was Madeleine with a foreign-sounding last name.

He picked two postcards from a rack at the front of the shop. The first picture was a tapestry of two knights on horseback in front of a castle. He read the caption on the back. *Jousting Knights, 1601, Morgan Moonstone, Medieval Tapestry Collection, Galleria dell'Accademia, Florence.*

The picture on the other postcard was also a tapestry. The back of the card said *Stag in the Forest, 1602, Morgan Moonstone, Medieval Tapestry Collection, Metropolitan Museum of Art, New York.*

Morgan Moonstone. The name was on both postcards. Was he an ancestor of the poet Vespera Moonstone? Had Morgan Moonstone woven the tapestries?

Will took the postcards to the counter and asked the boy for four red candles. He paid for his purchases, left the shop and headed up Black Penny Road with his bags. He was just about at Thom's door when Thom stuck his head out the window above and called, "What took you so long? Emma's here. We're going to set the Cherry Tart Flambé on fire!"

Will leapt up the stairs. Thom wore a flowered apron

and his hair was sticky with yellow custard. Emma was standing on her head in the middle of the room.

"How many seconds?" she grunted.

"Sixty-five," said a man with a pale face, seated in a wheelchair in front of a huge loom.

Emma collapsed on the floor. "Beat my record!" She had a long purple and red striped scarf draped around her neck. Will thought she looked amazing.

"Did you see Peaches on your way here, by any chance?" she said.

"No," Will replied.

The man in the wheelchair smiled. "You must be Will. I'm John, Thom's dad."

Will dropped his parcels on a table. He stood beside the loom and watched. John was weaving a picture of a lord and a lady riding a magnificent white stallion. The colours were vibrant – blue, gold and crimson. "It's awesome!" said Will.

"It's going to be a wall hanging," said John.

Will remembered his postcards. He took them out of a bag and showed them to the others. "I got them at a shop called *The Winking Cat*."

"That's my granny's shop!" said Emma. "She's too old to work there now, and we take turns looking after it for her. You must have met Lukas. He's one of my brothers."

"This one's my favourite," said Will, pointing to the postcard of the stag with silver antlers.

John wheeled over to have a closer look. "That's a very famous tapestry. The workmanship is exquisite. It's in the Metropolitan Museum of Art in New York."

"Who's Morgan Moonstone?" asked Will. "His name is on the back of both cards."

"What about the Cherry Tart Flambé?" interrupted Thom.

"Right," said John. "Into the kitchen, everyone! I want to see this too. And then we'll talk about Morgan Moonstone!"

Cherry Tart Flambé, Will discovered, was a big pie filled with pale yellow very lumpy custard.

"The lumps are the cherries," explained Thom. "I only had one can of cherries so I had to make a lot of custard."

Thom sprinkled sugar all over the pie. Then he stuck the pie under the broiler until the sugar turned a lovely brown. John produced a small bottle of something he called cognac. Thom poured the cognac over the pie. "Matches!" he said dramatically.

Emma handed him a box of matches. "Is there a fire extinguisher around here?" she asked.

"Very funny," said Thom.

"Stand back!" said John.

Thom lit the match and held it to the pie, which instantly burst into flames.

"CHERRY TART FLAMBÉ!" yelled Thom.

For a few breathtaking seconds, the flames shot up over their heads.

"Look out!" shrieked Emma.

Will thought the whole pie was going to burn up, but then, just as suddenly, the flames died down. Thom's breath came out in a whoosh. "It worked!" he cried. He did a little dance around the kitchen. "I am good. I am *soooo* good!"

They sat at the table and Thom dished it out with a giant spoon. Emma declared it was one of Thom's best desserts yet.

"*Hooo-whooo-hoooo,*" howled a voice from the street below.

"I'll let him in!" said Thom. He raced downstairs. Peaches bounded up ahead of him, a brown boot clamped firmly in his mouth.

"I can't get it away," panted Thom.

"It's old Mr. Branson's," said Emma. "That's the third time this week."

"Does he take things a lot?" said Will.

Emma nodded. "He's a retriever. Last week it was Mrs. Thompson's tablecloth and the Howard twins' baseball mitts."

Peaches dropped the boot and Emma grabbed it. "It's a full-time job taking everything back," she grumbled.

Will looked at John Fairweather. "Morgan Moonstone," he reminded him. "You were going to tell me about him."

"Right," said John. "Where should I begin? Over four hundred years ago a tapestry weaver came to Sparrowhawk Village. His name was Morgan Moonstone. He travelled with his wife and infant son."

"He wove magic tapestries!" said Thom.

"Is that true?" said Will. "Were they really magic?"

"Lots of people in this village believe it," said John. "They say that the tapestries could make things happen. You see, a tapestry tells a story. If a lord was planning a tournament, he would ask Morgan Moonstone to weave a magic tapestry showing his favourite knight winning, and then that knight *would* win!"

"Everybody would want a magic tapestry," said Will.

Would a magic tapestry have saved his mother? Would it make Mr. Barnaby publish *The Magical Night?*

CRAAASH! Emma and her chair toppled to the floor. Peaches leapt on top of her and washed her face with his slobbery pink tongue. "Hey! Get away!" said Emma picking herself up.

"I keep telling you not to tip back like that. Chairs are meant to stay on all four feet," said John. "We call Emma our jumping bean. Now, to get back to our story. Morgan Moonstone's tapestries are extremely valuable and today they're in museums all over the world. Like the ones in your postcards."

"Sparrowhawk is famous for its weaving," said Thom.

"You wait, any day now the first tour buses will arrive full of people looking for tapestries," said John. "Most of our best weavers are Moonstones, but even though their tapestries are splendid, they're not magic."

"You're a great weaver, too, Dad," said Thom, "and you're a Fairweather."

"And that's enough chatter for me or I'll never finish this tapestry." John wheeled his chair back to his loom.

"When are we going to look for the secret passageway?" asked Emma.

"What?" said Will. He was still thinking about magic tapestries.

"The secret passageway. Remember?"

"Right. I think I found the dungeon. I bought a torch so we can explore."

"Maybe we should clean up the kitchen first," said Thom quickly.

"I'll look after that," called out John.

"Chicken," taunted Emma.

Thom flushed. "I am not!"

"Then what are we waiting for?" said Emma.

chapter twelve

THE DUNGEON

))

THOM AND EMMA WAITED beside the suit of armour while Will took Aunt Mauve's packages to the Red Chamber. His aunt wasn't there, so he left them on the bed. He took the red candles to his tower.

He led Thom and Emma along the shadowy corridor to the heavy studded dungeon door. He tugged it open and flicked on the torch. He was the first down the steep dark steps, picking his way in the beam of light. The air smelled dank. Water dripped somewhere in the darkness. When they got to the bottom, Will waved the torch in a wide circle. They were in a large room with stained brick walls. A piercing squeal and the rustle of scurrying feet made everybody jump. *"RUFF!"* barked Peaches.

"A rat!" screeched Emma.

"It won't hurt you," said Thom. "It was more scared to see us. I'm sensing fear." He shuddered. "This place is mega-creepy. This is a bad idea. Let's get out of here!"

"How should we start?" asked Emma, ignoring Thom.

"Loose bricks," suggested Will. "Or maybe places where the bricks are a different colour."

He shone the light slowly across each wall. Iron rings were embedded in the old bricks. Pieces of chain lay scattered about on the uneven rocky floor. Rusty spikes stuck out of the back of an old wooden chair.

"Ohmigod!" said Emma. "This was a torture chamber!"

Thom moaned. Will swept the light into a corner. A sledge hammer and a metal rod lay on the floor. Someone had smashed the wall and pried out some of the bricks. Another wall of bricks lay behind. "Mr. Cherry's been in here!" he said. "I saw him sneaking that sledge hammer and that rod thing into an old shed behind the castle."

A low growl rumbled from Peaches' throat and the hair bristled on his back. They swung around. A lantern blazed at the top of the stairs but it was impossible in the glare to see who was holding it.

A voice sneered, "Oh, my. What do we have here?"

Mr. Cherry! He swung the lantern to the side, revealing his sallow face and long nose. He descended the stairs and waved his arm into the darkness.

"Having a look around, are you? The cells are over there. I suppose you've guessed what this room was used for? Torture! Sometimes I think I can hear the prisoners screaming."

Peaches barked. Mr. Cherry spat, "I warned you to keep that dog away from me!"

Emma slipped her hand under Peaches' collar.

"I was just making my rounds," said Mr. Cherry. "I said to myself, now who would have left that door open? Good thing I didn't lock it. You've heard that the castle is cursed? Just think of it. Three kiddies locked up in a dungeon forever. How tragic."

"Let's go," said Will in a loud voice.

"So soon?" said Mr. Cherry. "I haven't shown you the Duke's Tomb."

He swung the lantern over a hole in the floor. "There's a cell down there. They lowered the duke in with a rope. He didn't obey the king's orders."

Mr. Cherry licked his lips. "For twenty years, the duke was caged in there like an animal. His only entertainment was the screams of the tortured prisoners above him. They say he scratched a mark for every day on the wall. With his fingernails."

Peaches erupted in a frenzy of barking.

"Get out!" snarled Mr. Cherry. "Don't you dare come down here again! You or that scruffy dog!"

He turned to Will. "Brats who don't listen have a tendency to disappear forever."

Will forced himself not to run as he led the others up the stone stairs. Mr. Cherry breathed heavily behind them. He locked the studded door with a large key, attached to a brass ring and disappeared around a corner. No one spoke until they were safely in the tower.

"Whoa," said Emma. "He is one scary servant!"

"And now he's locked the dungeon door," said Will. "That messes everything up."

"Who cares?" said Thom. "Are you crazy? You couldn't pay me to go back down there. Hey! Look at that!" He pointed to the blue pencil box on the little round table. A faint golden light shone out from under the lid. "What is it?"

"A pencil box," said Will. "It does that sometimes. It was my mother's. She kept her writing pencils in it." For some reason, it had been easy to tell Favian about his mother, but now the words stuck in his throat.

"Can I open it?" said Thom.

Will nodded. Thom opened the box, and the light

faded away. "There's nothing in it except this," he said, picking up the piece of rolled-up cloth and the photograph of Will's grandparents. He turned the box upside down. "I don't get how it works. Is it some kind of magic?"

"It just does it," repeated Will.

Thom unrolled the cloth. He read out loud the words woven in delicate gold thread. "*The Griffin of Darkwood.* What's this?"

"Just something someone gave me," said Will.

"Let me see," said Emma. She studied it with interest. "Not a new tapestry. An old one."

Will had never thought that it might be from a tapestry. How had a piece of tapestry ended up with a photograph of his grandparents?

Emma picked up the photograph. "Who's this?"

"My mother and my grandparents," said Will.

"You look a little bit like your grandfather."

"His name was Sterling," said Will. "He was a writer. And my grandmother was a dancer. Her name was Carmelita."

"I wish the box would make that light again," said Thom. He put the strip of cloth and the photograph back inside and closed the lid.

"We need to look for the secret passage when Mr. Cherry's not here," said Emma. She flipped onto her hands and walked in a circle.

"He goes out sometimes," said Will, "but I never know when he's coming back."

"Let's just forget it," said Thom. "We could go back to my house and look up recipes or something."

"I'll come later," said Will. First he wanted to go back to Lantern Lane to have another look at the cat, Macavity.

chapter thirteen

TEA LEAVES

☽

WILL HEARD A CLINKING, clanking sound as he walked along Lantern Lane. He spun around. The Muses were following him.

"It's no use!" he shouted. "You might as well leave me alone. You won't inspire me any more. I'm never writing again!"

He started to run and was gasping for breath by the time he got to Vespera Moonstone's house. Vespera, wearing a blue batik skirt and several long ropes of wooden beads, answered his knock. Her deep brown eyes were welcoming.

"Will Poppy! I've heard about you from Favian. You must come in."

Vespera's house was untidy. Papers, books, pens and empty teacups were strewn across every surface in the front room. Macavity was stretched out on a rug in front of a gas fireplace. To Will's disappointment, his eyes were shut. Several cardboard boxes in the middle of the floor overflowed with copies of slim purple books with the title *A Mystical Muse* on the cover. Vespera had been in the middle of unpacking. "This is my newest book. I ordered more copies from my publisher. I never know how many

69

will sell when I do a reading."

"I came here this morning," said Will. "And...um...
your cat. I'm pretty sure I saw his eyes change colour."

"They have a tendency to do that," said Vespera.

"That's amazing!"

Vespera looked closely at Will. "Do you believe in
magic?"

"Yeah, I do!"

"Good. If you keep your eyes open, you'll find all
kinds of magic in Sparrowhawk. This is an ancient village. Now I'm going to make some tea and we'll have a
proper visit."

Vespera Moonstone disappeared. Will knelt down
beside Macavity, but the cat was still fast asleep. In a few
minutes, Vespera returned with a tray of cups and
saucers, a little pot of honey and a teapot. She poured the
tea, which she declared was from China. "None of the
cheap Indian teas for me. Too many bits of twigs for
properly reading tea leaves."

While Will stirred a spoonful of honey into his tea,
Vespera said, "Favian Longstaff told me the story of your
mother and Mr. Barnaby. He said that you're a writer too."

"I *was*," Will corrected her. "I don't write any more."

"Oh, but that doesn't mean you're not a writer," said
Vespera. "Once I didn't write a single word for five whole
years."

"Why didn't you write? Did your Muse desert you?"

"So you know about Muses, do you?"

"My Muse won't leave me alone. And my mum's
Muse is bugging me too. They want me to write. But I
won't."

"Really? Well, I think maybe I was afraid to write.

And then one night I woke up at two o'clock with a poem in my head that was begging to get out."

Vespera peered into Will's cup. "Save a little of your tea and I'll read your tea leaves. But first, tell me what kinds of things you like to write about."

In between sips of tea, Will told Vespera about his latest novel with the Knights of Valour and the Knights of Death. "The problem is, I never finish anything. I get partway through, and then I get another idea and I want to work on that instead. And now –" His voice broke off. He didn't know if he wanted to keep talking about it.

"Well, I think the Knights of Death and Valour sound intriguing," said Vespera. "It might be the novel you're meant to write. I think you should bring it back to life."

"I'm not planning to," said Will. "I hate the thought of writing now."

When he had a drop of tea left in the bottom of his cup, he gave it to Vespera who swirled the cup around and around three times. Carefully, she tipped it over the saucer. She waited a minute and then turned the cup right side up. Will peered at the wet tea leaves spattered inside the cup. "It doesn't look like anything."

"It's like seeing pictures in clouds. You can't rush it. We'll wait until they tell us your story."

Macavity got up from his spot in front of the fire and walked over to Will and bumped against his leg. Will reached down and stroked him. The cat's eyes remained a steady pale green. Vespera sat very still, staring into the tea cup, and Will wondered if she had gone into some kind of trance.

Finally, Vespera looked up. "I see a violin. You feel lonely sometimes."

"Yeah. I really miss my mum."

"Of course you do. Ah...several more pictures are becoming clear. I see some bumblebees, which means that you have been meeting new friends."

"Thom and Emma. I just met them yesterday, but it's kind of weird. It feels like I've known them forever."

"The best kind."

"What else do you see?"

"A boat. Someone important is coming to visit you soon. This person has been away but hasn't forgotten you."

"Mr. Barnaby! He's the man who's supposed to publish my mother's book."

Vespera passed her hand over the teacup. "You have very busy tea leaves." A sudden frown crossed her face.

"What is it?"

"I could be mistaken...yes, I'm sure I am...I think we'd better stop."

"You can't stop now! That's not fair!"

chapter fourteen

THE GRIFFIN'S CURSE

)

"THERE ARE TWO IMAGES here that are disturbing," said Vespera. "Two lizards. That almost always means hidden enemies and treachery."

"That's gotta be the Cherrys!" said Will.

"I wish I could say they were something else," sighed Vespera, "but there is no doubt in my mind that I'm seeing lizards...well, now this is interesting."

"What?"

"A hammer. Very rare. I believe it's telling us that you will triumph over adversity.'

"Adversity. I'm not sure what that means exactly."

"Great misfortune. Your life is not easy. But you will triumph, Will. That should give you hope."

Vespera and Macavity came outside with Will to the courtyard to say good-bye. Macavity rolled on his back on the brightly coloured tiles. Will frowned. "It's weird, but when I came here before I'm sure the tiles made a rainbow. Now they look like stars. Do you think that was magic?"

"Without a doubt," said Vespera. "A rainbow indeed. Have you been up to mischief, Macavity?"

Macavity contemplated his mistress with his slanted green eyes. They slowly turned a soft violet.

"There!" said Will. "See?"

"He's showing off," said Vespera. "Now you come back, William Poppy. You don't mind if I call you William, do you? It's a rare treat to find someone to talk to about writing. And try not to worry about your tea leaves."

✳

When Will got back to the castle, he went to the kitchen and asked Mrs. Cherry for a bucket of water and a rag. He tried to scrub the words GO AWAY off the front door, but it was no use. The letters blurred together but stubbornly refused to disappear. You could still tell what they said. How could anyone hate them that much? It didn't make any sense.

That night, he found some matches in the dining room and four saucers for candlesticks. He melted a blob of wax on each saucer, and stuck candles in all four and set them on the ledges in the tower wall. The lit candles cast long flickering shadows on the stone birds. He thought about the word *adversity*. He opened his trunk and took out his thesaurus and looked it up.

"*Difficulty, ordeal, hard times, ill wind, evil day, curse,*" he read out loud.

Curse! What if Vespera had made a mistake? What if he wasn't going to triumph? He stored the word *adversity* in his brain where he kept interesting words and then lay on his back on the bed and stared at the sparrowhawks. Who had carved them? He read for a while and then glanced at the candles. They burned brightly and looked just as tall as when he first lit them. Were they magic candles?

He thought about the weaver Morgan Moonstone, the tiles that changed from a rainbow to stars, Macavity's amazing eyes, Mr. Tumnus in the bookstore and the strange light that glowed in the pencil box. And now the candles. There was magic all around him. He put the thesaurus back in his trunk and picked up the writing book with the emerald cover, feeling an ache deep inside. Then he put the book back too.

Favian had said, "Once a writer, always a writer." He was wrong. Will knew he would never write again.

❋

In the morning, he went straight to Thom's flat. He knocked on the door and Thom opened it, holding a half-eaten peanut butter and jelly sandwich. John Fairweather was busy at his loom. "Hello, Will. Are you hungry? Thom has told me about Mrs. Cherry's cooking."

"Starving," said Will.

"Come on in the kitchen and I'll make you a pb and j sandwich," offered Thom.

While they were eating, John wheeled into the kitchen and poured himself a cup of coffee.

"I need to find out more about the griffin's curse," said Will. "Was there really a griffin?"

John sighed. "I suppose Thom and Emma told you about the girl who died in the castle."

Will nodded.

"Well, I hope they didn't alarm you. It happened years and years ago."

"Who was she?"

"Hannah Linley. Hundreds of years ago the king gave the Linleys the castle as a reward for good service. Over the years there have been a great many Lord Linleys."

"Hannah's grave is in the Linley graveyard," said Thom.

"Hannah was my dad's cousin," said John, "but I never knew her. She died before I was born. I've been told she was like Thom. She felt the suffering of animals. Her mother was a Fairweather who worked as a maid in the castle. Her father was Lord Linley. It must have caused quite a scandal. Hannah was brought up in the castle."

John took a sip of coffee. "Hannah inherited her gift with animals from the Fairweathers. When you read the dates on her gravestone, you realize she was no older than you when she died."

"Favian told me he had a friend called Hannah," said Will, "but he never told me she died. What happened to her?"

"She was very ill. I don't know anything else. It was forty years ago. Lord and Lady Linley left after she died and the castle was closed. Some people in the village believe that Hannah died because a griffin cursed the castle hundreds of years ago."

Thom said softly, "The mine, Dad. People blame the griffin's curse for the mine too."

"Yes, they do." John's eyes took on a distant look. "Ten years ago, the village got permission from the Linleys to open the castle and have a magic festival. They thought it would bring in tourists. The same night, the mine collapsed. People said it was because we opened up the castle and made the griffin angry."

"Maybe you shouldn't talk about it, Dad," said Thom.

"It's okay. A beam fell on me and I lost the use of my legs, Will, but at least I was spared my life. Twenty-four men died."

"Other bad things have happened too," said Thom. "Right, Dad?"

"There's stories of a dam breaking and washing away fifty homes in the seventeen hundreds, an epidemic of smallpox in the eighteen hundreds, a Linley who went insane seventy-five years ago and terrorized the village." John sighed. "And other stories too. People always blame the castle and the griffin. But none of that means that there's a curse."

"That's why the bus driver, Purvis Sneed, said we should stay away," said Will. "No one wants us in the castle! People are afraid of another disaster."

"Don't worry about Purvis Sneed," said John. "Most of us are pleased to see the castle lived in again. You mustn't pay attention to what people say."

"That's what Vespera Moonstone said when we were on the bus. But it's really scaring me."

"Griffins are a figment of our imaginations," said John firmly. "The castle is just what it appears to be – an old ruin. I'm delighted that your aunt has bought it. It's time we got rid of these superstitions."

But Will saw a shadow pass over John's face. *He's just trying to make me feel better,* he thought uneasily. *He does believe in the griffin's curse.*

chapter fifteen

SHADOW ALLEY

☾

WILL AND THOM LEFT the flat and walked to the book-store. When they got to the square, Peaches trotted past them carrying a big black umbrella. Vespera Moonstone was going out the door of *EX LIBRIS* just as they went in.

"Favian and I were finalizing some of the details for my poetry reading," she said. "We're thinking of serving cream puffs with vanilla ice cream and chocolate sauce. People will come if there's free food."

"Cream puffs!" said Thom. "They're in *Mastering the Art of French Cooking*. They have a fancy French name but it means cream puffs! I've been dying to try them. I'll make them for your reading!"

"Splendid," said Vespera.

Favian was on his knees, unpacking a new shipment of *The Lord of the Rings* trilogy.

"I've thought of two palindromes for you," said Will. "*Dad* and *did*. I know they're pretty lame but –"

"It's a start," said Favian. "It's much harder than you'd think. I had an inspiration last night. *Was it a cat I saw?* I might enter it in the next contest."

"What are you guys talking about?" asked Thom.

Will was explaining palindromes to him when *Thud!*

behind a tower of books, a volume hit the floor. A faint voice said, "Whoops."

Will and Thom spun around. The girl dressed all in black with long red hair and huge round glasses appeared around a corner. Will's eyes narrowed. *Her again!* It gave him the creeps how she kept popping up wherever he was.

"Are you on your way now, Madeleine?" said Favian. The girl mumbled something under her breath and fled.

"That was Madeleine de Luca," said Thom. "She's really weird." He frowned. "I hope she's not spying on us!"

"Why would she?" asked Will. "What's the matter with her?"

"I dunno. I told you, she's weird. She's home-schooled, and she's kind of snobby. Emma can't stand her."

They each found a book. Thom plopped into the saggy armchair, which had been moved to another corner of the shop. Will sat on the floor and leaned against the arm. He glanced up once into a pair of round green eyes peering at them between two piles of books. He instantly recognized Harry Potter's house elf. "Thom," he said in a low voice. "Look."

"What?" said Thom. "I don't see anything."

The face vanished. "Never mind," said Will.

"Dobby's here too," he told Favian on their way out.

"Excellent," said Favian.

Rain was spitting on the cobblestones of the square as they started up Black Penny Road. Brakes squealed in front of them and Mr. Cherry's pink van pulled over at the entrance to Shadow Alley. Will yanked Thom back into a doorway. Mr. Cherry got out of the van and slunk off down the alley.

"Let's follow him and see where he's going," said Will.

Thom chewed his lip. "I don't know –"

"We can always take off if we have to. Come on!"

Will strode into the gloomy alley and, with a sigh, Thom followed him.

It was as dark as night in Shadow Alley. Inky shadows filled the nooks and corners. Only a narrow strip of grey sky was visible between the tall soot-blackened buildings. Three scrawny alley cats were fighting over a discarded fish head and a dog, missing a front leg, limped past without giving the cats a glance.

"I'm picking up a lot of bad feelings in this alley," moaned Thom. "In my whole life I've never come in here. Now I know why."

His heart thudding, Will squinted through the gloom for any sign of Mr. Cherry. The alley was so narrow that in places you could almost touch the buildings on both sides. Low doors were set back in the grimy brick walls. Some of the windows had iron grills across them or wooden shutters nailed tight.

Shadow Alley would be perfect in a story, he thought. He turned and glanced back over his shoulder. The Muses were there, but very faint, like ghosts. *They're getting weaker*, he thought hopefully.

The alley climbed steeply. The rain had turned into a cold steady drizzle, and the slippery black cobblestones gleamed. A dark figure disappeared around a dim corner in front of them. Mr. Cherry. Will grabbed Thom's arm.

They waited for a few minutes and then crept around the corner. Mr. Cherry was gone. They were standing in front of a low curved door with a chipped tile above it that said *P. Sneed.*

"P. Sneed," whispered Will. "That must be Purvis, the bus driver."

"Mr. Cherry's gone inside," said Thom. "Let's get outta here."

Suddenly two long thin arms shot out of a dark recess beside the door. One bony white hand grabbed Thom's collar and the other grabbed Will's jacket.

They twisted and turned, trying to break away.

"Help!" yelled Thom. "Somebody save us!"

"No one will hear you in Shadow Alley," a voice hissed. "Unless perhaps it's a rat!"

chapter sixteen

BRUSSELS SPROUTS AND LIVER!

☽

"SNOOPING AGAIN!" growled Mr. Cherry.

"We're looking for Peaches," stammered Will. It was all he could think of. "He ran up here somewhere." He tried not to look at Mr. Cherry, but he couldn't help it. The man's eyes were eerily hypnotic.

"Never saw him. But good riddance. A lot of things go into Shadow Alley and don't come out."

"I've lived in this village all my life and I've never heard that," said Thom. He gave a desperate wrench and twisted out of Mr. Cherry's grasp. "Run!" he yelled.

Will delivered a swift kick to Mr. Cherry's shin. Curses exploded from the man and Will broke free. As he and Thom raced away, Mr. Cherry shouted, "Next time you DIE!"

Will and Thom were gasping when they got back to Black Penny Road.

"I thought we were goners," moaned Thom, shaking raindrops out of his messy hair.

"He must have been going to visit Purvis Sneed," said Will, remembering the conversation he had heard in the Cherrys sitting room. "The Cherrys are looking for something. It's got to do with the secret passageway. I think Purvis Sneed is helping them. The girl, Hannah, knew about it too. But what could it be?"

Thom shuddered. "Let's go. We're having Apple Charlotte! I made it this morning."

"Okay." Will had no desire to run into Mr. Cherry again today.

Will made the pb and j sandwiches while Thom boiled a mixture of apricot jam, sugar and a splash of his dad's dark rum to make sauce for the Apple Charlotte. Then he took a tray covered with tinfoil from the freezer and stuck his head into the living room. "Shepherd's pie okay?"

"Wonderful," said John.

Thom took off the foil and popped the tray in the oven. "Emma's mum, Star, makes frozen meals for Dad. She brings them over every Sunday. There's pork chops and liver and onions and beef stew left for this week."

They ate at the kitchen table. Thom had baked the Apple Charlotte in a round tin with a hole in the middle. "It's called a mold," he said. "I haven't used a mold before. When I flip it over on a plate, the Apple Charlotte will fall out. At least that's the plan."

When it was time to flip the mold, Will held his breath. The Apple Charlotte didn't budge. Thom tapped the bottom of the pan and peered underneath to see what was happening.

"Bang it harder," suggested John.

Thom whacked the bottom of the pan with a knife. "It's stuck," he said. He consulted his *Mastering the Art of French Cooking*, which was propped up against a canister of flour, open to the Apple Charlotte page. "Oh, no! I forgot the butter."

"We'll eat it out of the pan," said John.

They each had three huge helpings, scraping up the stuck bits. When they were finished, they pushed the dishes to the side and played gin rummy.

When it was time for Will to go, Thom said, "I'm going to make cream puffs tonight. I'm practising for Vespera's poetry reading. You can have some for breakfast tomorrow. You're gonna come, aren't you?"

Will promised. When he got outside, shiny puddles lay in all the dips in the road. In one puddle shone the reflections of glittering stars. He tilted his head back and gazed up at the sky. It was like a black blanket with not even one twinkling star. He took another look at the reflection in the puddle. The stars winked at him.

There's magic everywhere, he thought. *You just have to keep your eyes open for it.* He looked in every puddle the rest of the way but saw nothing so splendid again.

Ke-ke-ke-ke. The sparrowhawks circled the tower, screeching, as he entered the castle through the stone archway. In the entrance hall, the door to a closet where the phone was kept was partly closed. From inside the closet, Aunt Mauve shrieked, "Pepperoni, pineapple, double cheese...What do you mean, you don't deliver? How can you be a pizza parlour and not deliver?"

She slammed the phone down and emerged from the closet. She was wearing her coat, the wool scarf and three pairs of wool socks. Mrs. Cherry appeared from nowhere, her shoes making no sound on the stone floor. "Was there something wrong with the liver and Brussels sprouts I served for dinner, Madame?"

Aunt Mauve quivered under Mrs. Cherry's icy eyes. "Wha...no...nothing..." she mumbled.

"Why on earth would you phone a pizza parlour at

this time of night?" persisted Mrs. Cherry. "Is there a problem?"

"It was a wrong number, that's all."

Aunt Mauve sidled past Will. "What are you staring at?" She disappeared down a dark corridor.

"She won't get back to the Red Chamber that way," said Mrs. Cherry. "It leads to a deserted part of the castle."

For the first time ever, Will saw Mrs. Cherry smile. With a stomach satisfyingly full of scrumptious Apple Charlotte, he shot up to his tower.

chapter seventeen

THE CRYSTAL BALL

☽

THE NEXT MORNING, as Will was leaving the castle, a bell rang from the dining room. With a heavy sigh, he turned around and went to see what Aunt Mauve wanted.

She was hunched over one end of the long table, attempting to eat with mittens. A watery poached egg quivered in a bowl, and the chewed remnants of burnt toast were scattered about.

"Good morning," she said. In spite of the dreadful meal, she sounded cheerful, and Will was instantly suspicious. He stared at a pile of letters on the table beside the poached egg. His aunt swept them into her lap.

"Is that the post?" Will asked. "Where did it come from?"

"Mr. Cherry brought it up from the village. It's the only useful thing he's done since we got here."

"Is there anything for me?" Will hadn't totally given up on Mr. Barnaby yet.

"Who would write to you?"

Will didn't believe her. He glimpsed the end of a long white envelope peeking out of the pile. It looked just like the white envelope that had come to Aunt Mauve's house in the city.

Aunt Mauve pushed her chair closer to the table. A colourful brochure dropped to the floor and Will grabbed it. *"Fun in the Sun Cruises,"* he read. "Who's that for?"

"None of your beeswax!" crowed Aunt Mauve.

She picked up a big brass bell and rang it vigorously. "What's the point of having servants if they don't serve?"

"I'll go. What is it you want?" Will wanted to ask Mr. Cherry if any of the letters were for him.

"Tell Mrs. Cherry I insist on a new breakfast at once," said Aunt Mauve boldly. "Something I can eat this time. And I want the fire lit in the Red Chamber. It's always freezing in there!"

Will passed Cookie in the narrow passageway. He was muttering, "Spoiled! I put in too much salt!"

"Never mind," said Will. "It's not the end of the world."

Will almost lost his nerve at the kitchen door. He could hear voices. Good. Mr. Cherry wouldn't hurt him if there were other people around. And he had to find out about the post. He took a deep breath and pushed the door open.

He found Mr. Cherry and Mrs. Cherry sitting at the kitchen table. A fire crackled and snapped in the big stone fireplace. They had a guest – Purvis Sneed. He eyed Will gloomily. Plates with the remains of bacon, eggs, sausages and fried potatoes were pushed to one side. They were playing poker.

"What do you want?" asked Mrs. Cherry.

"Were any of the letters addressed to me?" asked Will.

Mrs. Cherry slapped her cards on the table and fixed her mean eyes on him. "Are you accusing Mr. Cherry of reading someone else's letters?"

"No! I just thought he might have noticed the envelope."

"I'm not a snoop," Mr. Cherry barked. "Unlike some people I know."

Purvis Sneed leered at Will. Bits of bacon protruded from between his teeth.

Will tried one more time. "It would have said Barnaby Book Publishers on the envelope. If it did, you should have given it to me."

Dead silence met his words.

"Oh, forget it," he sighed.

On his way out of the castle, Will took the shadowy corridor past the dungeon door. He tried the heavy door, but it was locked. Would he ever have a chance to go down there again?

✣

Will had walked all the way to Thom's building when he remembered that Aunt Mauve had asked him to order a new breakfast. "Serves her right!" he said with a grin.

He found Thom in the kitchen, surrounded by dirty dishes.

"Disaster!" said Thom. "The cream puffs. Hard as rocks. Even Peaches wouldn't want one. I've had to throw them all away. I don't know what I'm going to do. I'm running out of time!"

They filled up on pb and j sandwiches instead. Thom looked worried. "Are you getting sick of peanut butter?"

"Not yet," lied Will.

Then they went to Emma's house, a converted apple barn at the edge of the village. Emma and Peaches were on the grass in front of the house. Peaches had a piece of yellow rope tied to his collar and Emma hung onto the other end about ten steps away. "Peaches, come!" she said.

Peaches sat down.

"COME!" Emma tugged on the rope, and Peaches slithered on his bottom toward her.

"Peaches, DOWN!"

The dog flopped onto his tummy with a huge sigh.

Emma's mouth dropped open. "Hey! Did you see that? He did it!"

Will and Thom cheered and Emma gave Peaches a crisp from the bag she'd been munching from. Peaches swallowed it in one bite, gave a huge bark and sprang to his feet.

"STAY!" cried Emma, grabbing the end of the rope, but Peaches galloped across the grass, leapt over a low stone wall and disappeared.

They sat on the grass and ate the rest of the crisps and then Emma said, "Come on inside."

The barn still had a sweet cidery smell from the apples, which had been stored in it long ago. Huge black timbers crossed the ceiling and a balcony ran right around the large open room. Toys were scattered everywhere and drums throbbed from an upstairs room.

Emma's mother, Star, was feeding a baby at a high chair. "Welcome to Sparrowhawk," she said.

There were Storms everywhere. Will counted one, two, three...seven children. The drums stopped and a teen-aged boy with dreadlocks rattled down the stairs and out the door, grabbing a piece of toast on the way. It was Lukas from *The Winking Cat*. He slammed the door behind him.

From the corner of the room, a raspy voice demanded, "Bring the boy to me at once, Emma."

Will looked around in surprise. A tiny woman sat

behind a large wooden loom. Two sharp eyes peered at him. Her snowy white hair stood out like a halo around her wrinkled face.

"This is my great-grandmother," said Emma. "Granny Storm, this is Will."

"The boy from the castle. You remind me of someone, but I can't think who. It's your chin. Come up to my room so we can talk in private."

Will stiffened. The old woman looked strange and he didn't especially want to be alone with her.

"You've had some troubled times," Granny Storm added. "I see a dark aura around you. You're going to need a lot of courage in the days ahead."

"You'll give him the willies!" said Star. "You mustn't let Granny Storm scare you, Will."

"It's better to be prepared," muttered the tiny woman. "Will and I will go upstairs now. No one is to disturb us."

"You'd better go," said Emma. "She won't give up."

Granny Storm glared at her great-granddaughter and said, "Come with me."

Will followed Granny Storm up a wide flight of stairs to the balcony and then up another narrower steep flight of stairs that ended at a little door. When he walked through the door, he gasped. Light flickered from a dozen tall blue candles. The room was a hexagon. Magnificent tapestries hung on the walls, teeming with gleaming knights on charging horses, ladies and lords, deer, rabbits, pheasants, a leaping leopard and a prancing unicorn.

Just then there was a loud rustle of feathers. A sparrowhawk, sitting on a wooden perch, blinked its golden eyes.

"That's Prospero," said Granny Storm. "He has a

nasty temperament, but I'm fond of him."

She opened a latch on a small round window and swung it open. Prospero soared across the room and flew out. "He's after some supper," said the old woman, shutting the window. "He'll tap when he wants in again."

But Will barely heard her. He had forgotten his nervousness. He knelt in front of a low table that was covered with a purple velvet cloth. A candle flame flickered and danced on a silvery-grey glass ball on an ebony stand.

"Is this a real crystal ball?"

"Yes."

"Can I touch it?"

"Don't be rough."

He placed his fingers gently on the ball. It was ice-cold. Will held his breath and stared into its depths.

The old woman seemed to make up her mind about something. "Don't try so hard. Let the image come to you."

Just when he thought nothing was going to happen, milky colours began to swirl in the ball – pale reds and yellows and blues. A face floated into view. It was a man with haunted black eyes. Will knew him right away. "It's my grandfather, Sterling. He looks just like in my photograph."

"Did you say Sterling?" asked Granny Storm sharply. "It's an unusual name. I've only known one Sterling and that was forty years ago."

"Yes, but oh, he's disappearing. Do you think he wanted to tell me something?"

"How much do you know about him?"

"Not much. I don't even know his last name. My mother said he was a writer."

"Sterling," the tiny woman mumbled. "This boy looks just like him."

It was almost as if Granny Storm had known his grandfather. Will's eyes were pulled back to the crystal ball. The colours swirled, making him feel dizzy. Sweat prickled his back.

"It's awfully hot in here," he muttered.

The ball started to spin, faster and faster. He thought his head was going to explode. In a panic, he searched for Granny Storm, but the room was full of purple mist and he couldn't see her. Clammy fingers of mist touched his cheeks and seeped into his ears.

He was cold now, ice-cold.

"Help!" Will squeezed his eyes shut.

chapter eighteen

THE WHITE ENVELOPE

)

When Will dared to open his eyes, the ball had disappeared. He was in a clearing at the bottom of a steep gully. Dark trees, grey moss hanging in tatters from their limbs, crowded him on both sides. An overwhelming stench filled the air.

A deer lay on its back, its legs splayed crookedly and one milky eye staring up at him. He gasped in horror. The deer's stomach was torn open, and its entrails spilled onto the ground. Flies buzzed over the carcass.

The surrounding bushes were trampled and crushed, and ferns were flattened as if a huge creature had passed through. Then Will spotted bones, hundreds of them, picked clean and tossed aside. He was in the middle of a killing ground. Something fed here. The carcass was steaming and, with a sickening lurch, he realized he had disturbed some creature in the middle of its meal.

His eyes darted around wildly, looking for an escape. He tried to scramble up the side of the gully, reaching for a root to pull himself up. His hand slipped and a jolt of pain stabbed his knee. He grabbed a handful of ferns to stop himself from sliding back down.

Just then, a roaring wind swept through the trees. Will looked back over his shoulder. A huge shadow dropped over him.

He threw himself sideways. His head banged against something hard. Everything went black.

⁂

When Will opened his eyes, Granny Storm was peering down at him. A veil of purple vapour hung in the air above her.

Will sat up and rubbed his throbbing head. "What happened?"

"You banged your head on the table leg."

"I mean before that."

"You entered the ball. I've never heard of anyone doing that on their first time."

Will stood up slowly. His mouth was dry and his legs wobbled. He felt drained. Something warm dripped down his leg. He looked down at his right knee. There was a hole ripped in his jeans, the edges soggy with blood.

The crystal ball was ordinary now, still and dull grey.

"What did you see?" demanded Granny Storm.

"I can't talk about it." Will thought he was going to throw up.

"You're as white as a sheet. The ball has that effect. We need to talk."

"I won't," said Will. "I have to go."

⁂

"You went into the ball!" guessed Emma.

"Oh, Will," said Star. "I've told Granny Storm over and over –"

"It's okay," said Will hoarsely. "I'm okay."

Emma's brothers and sisters were staring at him. He was desperate to leave. But how was he going to make it as far as the castle? It seemed miles and miles away.

"I've got to go home," he said. "Come on, Thom."

"I'll come with you guys," said Emma.

"You're babysitting little Jeremy King in half an hour," said Star.

"Unfair!" cried Emma. "I'll come as soon as I can."

Will barely heard her. He stumbled out of the house with a mumbled good-bye.

Bones...blood...an enormous shadow. What exactly had he seen?

�֍

When Will and Thom got back to the castle, they bumped smack into Aunt Mauve, who was heading out through the stone archway, wearing her purple boots and her squirrel cape. When he saw the squirrels, Thom turned white.

"Out of my way! I've no time to talk to you," said Aunt Mauve. "I'll miss my bus."

"What do you mean, bus?" said Will.

"If you must know, I'm going back to the city. I have urgent business to take care of. I'll be gone for two days."

It's because of that long white envelope, thought Will. He was still pondering the envelope when he and Thom went inside. He headed down a dim passageway. "Follow me!" he called.

Thom stopped dead in his tracks. "Where are we going?"

"The Red Chamber. Aunt Mauve's room. There's something I have to look for."

Will led Thom through the maze of passageways. They passed the door to the dungeon. This time it was partly open and they could hear the sound of something smashing. "Mr. Cherry's at it again," said Will. "I don't suppose we'll ever get another chance to look around in there by ourselves. I'd give anything to find out where he hides the key."

"Not me," said Thom.

Aunt Mauve had left the Red Chamber in a tremendous hurry. Scarves, stockings, hats and shawls were draped everywhere. Will started digging through the contents of a wastepaper basket full of wadded up tissues. "Aha!" He held up a scrap of torn envelope with a colourful Russian stamp in the corner.

The first long white envelope had come from Australia. And now Russia. Who would write to Aunt Mauve from so far away? And why?

He turned the wastebasket upside down and spilled its contents onto the floor. Thom kept glancing up at the door as he helped sort through the tissues for the missing pieces of envelope.

"Here's my name," said Will, examining a torn piece of paper. "*William Poppy.* I knew it!"

Soon they had a pile of white scraps. Will scooped them up and put them in his jacket pocket. "Let's get out of here," he said.

When they passed the dungeon door, it was shut, and the key was dangling in the lock. "Yes!" cried Will. "Mr. Cherry forgot to take the key!" He grabbed it and slipped it into his other pocket. "We'll come back later."

They sped up to the tower. Will spread the scraps of envelope on the floor and they went to work fitting them together.

"It's like a jigsaw puzzle," said Thom.

Will fit in the last piece. "Got it!"

The envelope said *Master William Poppy* and was addressed to Aunt Mauve's house in the city. Someone had written FORWARD across the top and the address of Sparrowhawk Hall. The return address in the top left corner said *Oliver Barnaby, Russia*.

Will seethed. How dare Aunt Mauve steal his letters! The first white envelope that had arrived in the city must have been for him too. And what was Mr. Barnaby doing in Russia?

"Aunt Mauve must have kept the letter that was inside," he said. "Maybe Mr. Barnaby was writing me about my mum's book. Now I'll never know if it was good news or bad news!"

"What book?" asked Thom.

Will hesitated, then poured out the story of his mother and Mr. Barnaby and *The Magical Night*.

"What are you going to do?"

"I don't know. Mr. Barnaby could be anywhere by now. It sounds like he's on a trip around the world. But one thing's for sure! As soon as Aunt Mauve gets back, I'll make her tell me the truth!"

chapter nineteen

AN OWL CALLED MINNIE

)

WILL WAS BACK INSIDE *Granny Storm's crystal ball. He felt himself falling...falling into the gully. The stench was every-where. The deer had become a pile of bleached bones. He picked up the skull and stared into the black empty eye sockets.*

To his horror, the jaw moved. "The curse," said the deer. "Escape while you can. Leave Sparrowhawk."

Will turned to run but he was encircled by a fence of bones. "You're doomed," chanted the bones. "You'll never get away."

Will's eyes snapped open. His heart raced. His eyes swept over the carved sparrowhawks, his mother's pencil box...he was safe in the tower.

He forced himself to stay awake until morning, terri-fied that the dream would come back. Finally, he climbed out of bed, stiff and cold, and pulled on his jeans and T-shirt. He stood on the bed and climbed through the trap door onto the roof. The village below slumbered in the early morning. He turned the other way and gazed at the forest, the trees packed so densely it was almost black. Was that where the magic ball had taken him? Was the gully of death hidden somewhere in those trees? The for-est had secrets. Will knew that for sure. Emma had said that no one ever went into it because of the curse. The deer skull had warned him about a curse in his dream. *Leave Sparrowhawk*, it had said.

"No," said Will out loud. "You can't scare me away. I won't go!"

A movement caught his eye. Someone was standing close to the towering oak tree with the SOLD sign. Madeleine de Luca! The sun winked on her big round glasses.

"What are you doing?" shouted Will.

Madeleine stared up at him and then turned and ran down the road.

"And stay away!" yelled Will. He was finally rid of the Muses – they hadn't been back since that day in Shadow Alley. The last thing he needed was a weird girl hanging around. He scrambled down through the trap door and set out down Black Penny Road to Thom's. He kept a sharp eye out for Madeleine, but she had disappeared.

Thom and Emma were in the kitchen. In the middle of the table, a tiny ball of bristly fuzz stared at Will.

"What is it?" asked Will.

"An owl," said Thom.

"Oh, wow! He's amazing!"

"It's a she," said Thom. "And she's not a baby. She's an elf owl. They're the smallest owls in the world. I looked it up in our bird book."

The owl was no bigger than Will's hand. She had white eyebrows and bristly feathers on her legs. "Where did you find her?"

"I was practising making cream puffs last night." Thom's face fell. "It's harder than it looks."

"The poetry reading's the day after tomorrow," said Emma.

Thom glared at Emma. "I know that."

"What about the owl?" asked Will.

"Right. I was just taking the cream puffs out of the oven when I heard this pecking sound at the window. I thought it was hail, but it went on and on and so I opened the window, and in she flew. I've named her Minnie because she's so small."

Minnie gave three little hops past the salt shaker. She fluttered her wings and landed on Thom's shoulder. Thom held his breath. He put his finger up and the little owl nibbled it gently with her beak. "*Tu-tu-tu*," she whistled.

"I think she's hungry," said Emma.

Thom looked worried. "The book says she eats scorpions."

"Where do you find scorpions around here?" asked Will.

"It's a problem," Thom admitted. "I hope she'll like grasshoppers."

"How about some pb and j sandwiches for us?" Emma suggested. "Don't move, Thom! I'll make them."

They ate at the kitchen table. Minnie perched on Thom's shoulder, her head swivelling back and forth.

"She sure doesn't act like a wild owl," said Emma. "I think she came to your window on purpose. Somehow she knew that you understand animals."

"D'you think so?" asked Thom.

"Okay, get this," said Will. "I've got the dungeon key!"

"I'm only going if Mr. Cherry's out," said Thom quickly.

Minnie rode on Thom's shoulder to the living room. He picked her up gently and set her in the jade tree, and

John promised to keep an eye on her. On the way up Black Penny Road, Peaches bounded out of an alleyway, howling with joy to find them. When they arrived at the castle, they climbed the spiral stairs to Will's tower.

Thom went straight to the pencil box. "It's not doing anything," he said.

Emma did a back bend and then peered out a window. "Mr. Cherry just left. The coast is clear."

Will retrieved the dungeon key from its hiding place in his trunk.

"I've changed my mind," said Thom. "I'll wait here. I'll be the guard in case he comes back."

He flopped on the bed and Peaches leapt up beside him. Will got his torch and he and Emma set off.

"Don't blame me if he kills you!" called Thom.

chapter twenty

A CLUE IN THE DUNGEON

))

"Mr. Cherry's smashed tons of bricks!" said Emma.

"But he's given up." Will scanned the cobwebby dungeon. "He's taken the tools away. He must be going to look somewhere else."

"Why?" Emma frowned. "What's he after?"

"That's what we have to find out." Will took one last look around and shuddered. It was horrible to imagine the prisoners' screams and the duke trapped in the hole in the ground.

"Wait a sec," said Emma. "Shine the light over there in that corner. I think I saw something."

Will turned the torch.

"What's this?" Emma bent down and picked up something on top of a pile of broken bricks. "It's your postcard!"

"What? Let me see."

Emma passed him a slightly crumpled postcard. He studied it in disbelief. It was the picture of the silver stag. He turned it over and read the inscription on the back. *Stag in the Forest, 1602, Morgan Moonstone, Medieval Tapestry Collection, Metropolitan Museum of Art, New York.*

"Mr. Cherry must have dropped it," he said slowly.

"I don't get it. How did Mr. Cherry get your post-card?"

"I don't know." Will felt sick at the thought of Mr. Cherry poking through his things in the tower. "I'm going back to check."

When they got back to the tower, Will went straight to the bag from *The Winking Cat* and dumped it out on the bed. Both postcards fell out.

"Mine's still here," he said, filled with relief and con-fusion. "Mr. Cherry must have bought one too. Why would he want a picture of an old tapestry?"

No one could think of an answer. Will stared at the matching postcards. It was an important clue, he was pos-itive, but he had no idea what it meant.

They spent the rest of the morning searching through empty rooms and passageways for the secret passage. Will ran out to the shed and got a hammer, and they tapped on walls and pressed against wood panels. They discovered a library and spent a discouraging hour pulling dusty books with dull titles off the shelves and peeking behind.

Will tried to find his way to the guard's walk so he could show his friends the long drop off to the river below, but he got hopelessly lost.

"Listen," said Thom once. "Do you hear someone crying?"

"It sounds like a boy," said Emma.

"The ghost!" said Will.

They abandoned their hunt for the secret passage and looked for the ghost instead, but every time they opened a door, certain they had found him, the sobbing moved somewhere else.

"It's no use," said Will finally. "We can't find the secret

passageway or the ghost!"

They separated outside the castle. Thom set off across the rocky valley in pursuit of grasshoppers and caterpillars for Minnie. Will walked with Emma and Peaches as far as *The Winking Cat* and continued on his own to the bookstore. The EX LIBRIS sign rattled in the wind. He opened the door and went inside. At the jingle of the bell, Favian looked up from his newspaper.

"Hey," said Will.

"You look like a man on a mission."

"I am, sort of. I need a book about griffins."

"Magical creatures would be a good place to start," said Favian.

"I'm trying to find out about something called the Griffin of Darkwood."

"Never heard of it. Let's see. Maybe a book about famous magical creatures in history."

Favian and Will squeezed up and down the aisles while Favian mused, "Let me see. It's around here somewhere."

"Did you see that?" asked Will suddenly.

"What? Perhaps it's with the –"

"Gandalf! He was just there, but he's gone now!"

"So Gandalf's showed up. Good eyes, Will! Ah! Here it is!" Favian pulled out a fat book with a glossy picture of a phoenix on the cover. "Why don't you look in here first?"

Will sat on the dusty floor and thumbed through the book. There were no pictures, and the type was tiny. An extensive index at the back didn't even include griffins. For the next hour, he skimmed through the tables of contents and indexes of dozens of books. He found lots of illustrations of griffins. The best was a griffin standing on top of a cliff, its huge wings stretched to the sky.

His eyes drifted over the shelves. A small scrap of paper was tucked between two books. He pulled it out. Someone had written on it in big block letters:

THE GRIFFIN OF DARKWOOD???

Somebody else wanted to know about the Griffin of Darkwood? But who?

Will hurried to the front of the shop.

"D–a–n–d–a. No! It doesn't work!" Favian looked up from his paper full of scribbled letters. "Find what you were looking for?"

"No."

"Madeleine De Luca's been looking at books about magical creatures too. She's been in and out of the shop for a week."

Madeleine De Luca! Could she have left the paper?

"I need to ask her something," Will said, "but I don't know where she lives."

"Number 40 Silk Alley. She lives in the back of *Carta da Lettere*. It's a stationery shop."

"I'll go right now! See ya later.'

"You bet," said Favian.

chapter twenty-one

MADELEINE DE LUCA

)

CARTA DA LETTERE WAS TUCKED away at one end of Silk Alley, a narrow street behind the square. The shop window was dark and a sign that said SORRY WE'RE CLOSED hung on the glass door.

Will pressed his face against the glass. A dim pinkish light glowed from a tall Tiffany lamp. A shadow moved across the back of the shop. He knocked on the door. He was sure that someone was standing there, frozen in the darkness. He knocked a second time, harder.

The shadow moved again and the door opened a crack. Madeleine de Luca's white face and round glasses peered out at him. "Can't you read? Go away!"

"Please. Just let me in for a minute."

"My parents aren't here. I *said* go away."

"Don't shut the door!"

Fear flashed across Madeleine's face.

"The Griffin of Darkwood. Does that mean anything to you?" asked Will.

Madeleine gasped. She opened the door just wide enough for Will to slip in.

"We'll go in the back," she whispered. She led Will through the dimly lit shop, past a display of old-fashioned glass ink bottles and quill pens in brass stands. They went into a little room behind the shop. It was stifling hot and crammed with spindly furniture. Madeleine twisted a strand of her long red hair. "What do you want?"

Will took the scrap of paper out of his pocket. "I think you wrote this and left it in the bookstore."

"What if I did? Is that a crime?"

"Someone gave me a piece of old tapestry. It says 'The Griffin of Darkwood' on it. I think it was my grandfather's."

Madeleine's mouth fell open. "Have you got any more pieces of the tapestry?"

"No. If you could tell me anything about the Griffin of Darkwood, it might help."

"You better come with me."

Her bedroom had a narrow bed with a black bedspread, black curtains, a round table spread with cards and a poster on the wall of a man dressed in black, riding a black horse. *Seriously spooky*, thought Will.

"It's in the cards," said Madeleine.

Will stepped over to the table. Cards were laid out on the table in three rows and other cards were stacked to one side. On the front of each card there was a detailed coloured picture and a title. Will forgot about Madeleine. He was drawn into the cards with their beautiful pictures. He read some of the names out loud, "Nine of Swords, Two of Wands, Queen of Pentacles, The Fool, Wheel of Fortune, the Joker, the Magician, Death." The picture on the Death card was a silver skull over a shield and a black flag with a strange white flower on it.

"What kind of cards are these?" said Will.

"Tarot cards." Madeleine chewed on her fingernail. All

her nails were bitten to the quick and her cuticles were red. "I got them at *The Winking Cat*."

"What are they for?"

"Divination. Predicting the future." She spoke quickly now. "There are seventy-eight of them. They can guide your life. I don't do anything without checking first with my cards."

Will was starting to wish he hadn't come. He had never met anyone like Madeleine before. What did the tarot cards have to do with The Griffin of Darkwood?

"You lay down what's called a spread," said Madeleine. "Five or seven cards at a time. You make a pattern. And then you turn them over and read the meaning."

She grabbed Will's arm, her fingers digging in sharply. Her words came in short bursts. "A card with The Griffin of Darkwood on it...it kept coming back...I told it to go away but it wouldn't!"

"I don't get it." Will yanked his arm away.

"I put eleven cards on the table. It's called the Celtic Cross. And when I turned the cards over, it was there. A card with a huge griffin on it and the words *The Griffin of Darkwood*! I'd never seen that card before."

She's scared out of her wits, thought Will.

"The card was so powerful. It engulfed every other card with its force. I thought I was going to faint. You can't imagine it if you haven't felt it yourself."

Will swallowed. "What did you do?"

"I tried again. The griffin card kept coming back. Finally, I tore it up. I lit a candle and burned all the pieces when the moon was shining. Then I buried the ashes. I'm convinced the card was trying to give me a message. I've been so worried I haven't been able to sleep."

She took a big shuddering breath. "It ruined the cards for me. I didn't even want to look at them for awhile. But that's not all. Something else happened."

"What?"

"On the same night that I burned the card, I asked my Ouija board for help. It spelled out a name. It was your name. Will Poppy. I didn't know who you were."

Will went cold with shock.

"Then I saw you at the bookstore, and I asked Favian who you were. Don't you see? You were fated to come here. The Griffin of Darkwood has a message for you. It tried to tell me through my tarot cards."

"I don't know what you mean."

"It's some kind of prophesy. We could ask the Ouija board. Right now. It won't take long."

"Forget it! I'm leaving."

"Please."

"No!"

"All right." Madeleine didn't say anything as they walked back through the shop to the front door.

"I'm going to keep looking in the books at the bookstore for The Griffin of Darkwood," said Will. "Someone must know something about it."

Madeleine shrugged. "I've finished reading most of those books. I've been going every day. There's nothing in them about The Griffin of Darkwood. But you can suit yourself."

With that, she shut the shop door firmly.

Feeling like he had escaped, Will sucked in gulps of the fresh cool air. He hurried back along Silk Alley toward the square and then up Black Penny Road. Something flew up the street and landed on the windowsill of Thom

Fairweather's flat. It was the tiny elf owl, Minnie, with a spider dangling from her beak.

Thom opened the window and the owl glided inside. He saw Will and shouted, "Bad news! I've burnt the cream puffs!" He shut the window and disappeared.

When Will got to the top of the hill, he stopped and stared at the ancient stone castle. The ruins of the huge keep loomed like a silent guard. The Griffin of Darkwood. It was somewhere close by, Will was convinced.

chapter twenty-two

A FAMILY TREE

☽

IN THE MORNING, Will took all his books back to EX LIBRIS and exchanged them for new ones. Favian was slitting the tape on a huge cardboard box that sat on the floor.

"A new book order?" said Will.

"Old books. Ebenezer Moonstone died last week. He was a hundred and eight! He had a collection of rare books and his grandson has packed them up and sent them to me. You can help me unpack if you like."

"Moonstone," said Will. "One of the magic weaver's descendants?"

"Yes, and a history buff like me. I've admired his collection for years."

Favian peeled back the flaps and a musty smell rose out of the box. They took turns lifting out books, exclaiming over the richly coloured leather covers embossed with gold letters. Soon, they were each absorbed in a book, Will's about medieval knights and Favian's a history of local folklore.

It was lunchtime before they stopped reading. Will poked his head deep into the box to make sure they hadn't missed a book. "There's something at the bottom."

He lifted out a sheet of paper. It was covered in a

spiderweb of black lines and names, written in tiny letters. Will spread the paper flat on the desk. "Look! Here's Vespera's name!"

"What have you there?" asked Favian, peering over his shoulder. "It looks like... Great heavens! It's Morgan Moonstone's family tree! Ebenezer told me he was working on it, but I never believed he could do it. He used old letters and family Bibles. People often recorded the names of all their children in their Bibles. It was a huge undertaking for Ebenezer!"

They studied the paper. The name Morgan Moonstone was written boldly at the top, and the lines of names all led back to his name. Will pointed out Vespera's name at the bottom. And then his heart thumped wildly. "Favian," he gasped. "There's me! See, *William*. And there's my mother, Adrienna!"

"Good Lord!" said Favian.

In a shaky voice, Will read out loud the names connecting him to Morgan Moonstone.

"Glenville, Kincaid, Rainart, Charles, Denton, Cyrus, Hyde, Lennox, Sterling, Adrienna, William!"

"Extraordinary!" cried Favian.

"Sterling was my grandfather! I have a photograph of my grandparents. I never knew his last name was Moonstone."

"Sterling Moonstone was a great friend of mine. Hannah, Vespera, Sterling and I played together when we were kids. And you are his grandson! I see the resemblance now. It's your chin. But who would have ever thought such a thing? Sterling left Sparrowhawk years ago, after –"

He stopped talking and squeezed his hands together.

"What an incredible coincidence that you and your aunt should move to this village."

"It wasn't a coincidence," said Will. "Aunt Mauve said it was like she was under some kind of spell when she bought Sparrowhawk Hall. I think that's true." He stared at Favian. "What does it mean?"

"I shall have to think on it," said Favian gravely. "But I am certain of one thing. There is a reason you have come to Sparrowhawk Hall. We just have to find out what it is."

❄

Will hurried straight to Thom's to tell him.

Thom was still in his pyjamas, Minnie perched on his shoulder. He had big dark circles under his eyes and his hair stuck up in clumps. He'd been tossing and turning most of the night, worrying about cream puffs. He listened to Will's story with his mouth hanging open. "You're a Moonstone! YOU'RE A MOONSTONE! This is like AMAZING! Dad, did you hear what Will said?"

"I did!" John had stopped weaving while Will talked and had listened with rapt attention. "It's incredible!"

"I know." Will could hardly believe it himself and he had seen his name right there on the paper. "Favian thinks there's some reason I'm here."

"Kind of like fate," said Thom. "Very cool!"

Will and Thom ate two pb and j sandwiches each for lunch, talking through mouthfuls about everything that had happened.

"I'm going over to Emma's to tell her," said Will. He figured he could stay out of Granny Storm's way.

"No point," said Thom. "She called this morning. She's grounded."

"What?"

"She's gotta help Granny Storm sort her yarns."

"What did she do?" asked Will.

"Dunno."

Will was surprised at how disappointed he felt. He'd been trying to picture Emma's face when he told her the news. Would she think it was a big deal like Thom did? He hoped so.

Thom yawned hugely. "I won't be able to help you look for the secret passage today. I'm going back to bed."

"All day?"

"Maybe."

Will sighed. "I'll see you later."

chapter twenty-three
A BROKEN PROMISE

☽

WILL SPENT PART of the day reading books at EX LIBRIS, with frequent breaks to pore over the family tree, and part of the day at Vespera's cottage. Vespera's nerves were a little rattled because of the poetry reading the next day. "Cooking will be a good distraction," she said. "How about some peanut butter pancakes for supper?"

"Peanut butter?" said Will, his heart sinking.

Vespera winked. "Blueberry, then, with lots of syrup and bacon."

By nighttime, Will's head was buzzing and it was impossible to go to sleep. He was a descendant of Morgan Moonstone, the magic tapestry weaver! He said the words out loud and a delicious chill ran down his spine. It was like something out of one of his beloved fantasy books! If only he could tell his mother!

At midnight, the four red candles burst into flame. He was getting used to strange things, but this made him jump. The shadows from the flickering flames danced across the carved stone birds. He sat up on the edge of the bed, thinking. At last he blew out the candles and crawled back under his blanket, finally drifting into a restless sleep. When he woke up, he looked at his watch. Ten o'clock! He couldn't believe how late he'd slept.

Will threw on his clothes and scrambled down the spiral staircase. Today was a perfect day! Vespera Moonstone was having her poetry reading tonight. And he, Will Poppy, was a Moonstone! All his fears and worries seemed to have slipped away in the night.

In his excitement, he crashed into Aunt Mauve, who was coming through the stone archway with a bag of shopping.

"You're back from the city!" said Will.

"Of course, I'm back. I arrived late last night. It's about time you got up. There are mice in this dreadful castle. They've tipped over my wastebasket and there are tissues everywhere. That useless Mr. Cherry is nowhere about. I've had to walk all the way to the village for mousetraps."

"Give me my letter," said Will.

An enormous sneeze exploded from Aunt Mauve. "I've got a horrible cold. It's this icebox of a castle. *Ah-choo!* The sooner we're out of here, the better."

"My letter from Mr. Barnaby."

"Whatever are you talking about? I saw your precious Mr. Barnaby in the city yesterday."

"You can't have. He's on a world tour."

Aunt Mauve snorted. "Where did you get that idea? He's in the city and he has no intention of publishing your mother's book."

"You're lying."

"He told me so himself. Ah-choo!"

Will ducked and took off at a run. How could he have thought it was such a perfect day? He despised Aunt Mauve. *Despised* her. And he hated Mr. Barnaby too. *That's* what the letter had been about. Mr. Barnaby had changed his mind. He wasn't going to publish *The Magical Night*.

Will ran down Black Penny Road. When he got to the shops, he had to dodge throngs of people carrying bags, some in a hurry and some stopping to gaze in interest at the ancient buildings. Shop doors stood open, and in the street tapestries were displayed on racks or hung on stone walls like exotic butterflies. Why were there so many people? What was going on?

On Thom's front door was a sign that said *Please come up. Tapestries for sale.*

John's tapestry was hanging on a wall inside the flat and several smaller ones were draped over the backs of chairs. John was in a navy blue suit and his curly hair was slicked back.

"What's happening?" asked Will.

"The tour buses are here," John told him.

"Get in here, Will!" yelled Thom from the kitchen.

Flour was strewn from one end of the kitchen to the other. Spilled milk dripped onto the floor and Minnie was pecking at a pile of broken eggshells.

"I think I've got it perfect this time," said Thom, hopping back and forth in front of the oven. He raced over to his *Mastering the Art of French Cooking* and read, "The puffs are done when they have doubled in size, are golden brown and firm and crusty to the touch."

He ran back to the oven and peered through the glass oven door. "They've gotten SMALLER!" he cried. "They've...COLLAPSED!"

Will ate six anyway, with jam, but Thom refused to touch them. "The poetry reading is tonight!" he cried. "What am I going to do?"

"Have you been outside?" asked Will. "Have you seen all the people?"

Thom groaned. "You're making me feel worse. They'll probably all come to the poetry reading. It's the tour buses. They're down in the square. They're the first ones. They'll come every week now." Thom rubbed his floury hands through his hair. "Dad's coming downstairs tonight. For the poetry reading. Emma's dad is coming to get him."

Minnie flew over to the table and Thom fed her a scrap of cream puff. Will licked the jam off his fingers and poured out the story of Mr. Barnaby and his broken promise.

"That's so unfair! I thought Mr. Barnaby was your friend," said Thom, forgetting for a moment about his cream-puff disaster.

"So did I."

"You can't give up. Why don't you ask Favian? He knows a lot about books. He'll know what to do."

"Great idea!" said Will. "Let's go and I'll help you make some more cream puffs later."

They left straightaway for EX LIBRIS.

chapter twenty-four

DEAR MR. BARNABY

)

FIVE LONG BUSES were parked at the end of the square. Tourists milled everywhere, wandering in and out of shops, licking ice-cream cones and taking photos.

Favian was dusting shelves in the bookstore. His eyes glowed with excitement. "I've made tremendous sales all morning. There's a lull right now. I'm hoping some tourists will stay for Vespera's reading tonight. We're having warm apple cider and your cream puffs, Thom. We're going to serve them with vanilla ice cream and chocolate sauce."

Thom groaned.

Favian put down his duster and listened while Will told him about Mr. Barnaby and *The Magical Night*.

"You must write a letter to this Mr. Barnaby," he said. "It's the only thing to do."

"What would I say?"

"Take the positive approach. Tell him the EX LIBRIS bookstore would like one hundred copies! That's sure to make him think."

One hundred copies! "Are you serious?", said will.

"Absolutely. ASAP. That's just for a start. I have total faith in your mother's book."

Favian burrowed into his desk and produced a sheet of thick cream-coloured writing paper. "Be courteous but firm," he advised. "You can do it. You're the writer."

Favian continued with his dusting and Thom read books while Will composed his letter. After much sighing and lip chewing, he was ready to read it out loud.

Dear Mr. Barnaby.

I am writing to you regarding my mother Adrienna Poppy's book The Magical Night.

Mr. Favian Longstaff, a successful bookseller, would like to place an order of ONE HUNDRED copies. I told him that you said that The Magical Night *will be a best seller. He promises to order more copies in the future. He asked me to tell you that he would like to receive the copies AS SOON AS POSSIBLE as he has many eagerly waiting customers.*

Yours truly,

William Poppy

P.S. What happened to the money?

P.P. S. My mother and I believed in you.

When Will got to the end, Thom said, "Perfect! You are a good writer. I wouldn't have known what to say."

"It's just a letter," said Will. "It's not like real writing."

"It needs an envelope and a stamp." Favian rifled through a few more drawers, humming. "Here we go."

Will wrote Barnaby Book Publishers Inc. and the address on the front of the envelope.

"I'm going to the post office at noon," said Favian. "I'll put it in the post box for you."

Favian sounded so optimistic that Will cheered up. He and Thom left the bookstore and headed to *The*

Winking Cat.

"Here comes Peaches," said Will, watching the dog, his mouth full of frothy pink lace, trot up the road. When they opened the shop door, Peaches slipped in behind them.

Emma was at the counter, busy wrapping a large turquoise stone in tissue paper. She glanced up and frowned. "Now what?" She pried open her dog's mouth and pulled out the pink lace and held it up. "It's a BRA!"

"Emma!" said Thom.

"Well, it is," said Emma.

"Maybe it's Star's?" said Will.

"No way," said Emma, stuffing it in a drawer. "He's raiding clotheslines again! I can't exactly go around asking people if they've lost a bra."

Her face brightened. "Thom told me you're a Moonstone! That means that you'll stay in Sparrowhawk!"

Had she been worrying that he would leave? Will felt his cheeks turn hot.

"It's amazing! It's the *best* news ever!"

"Not everyone's going to think so," said Will. He still felt sick when he thought of the words GO AWAY on the castle door.

"Phooey to them!" Emma rang up a purchase of purple candles for a big woman in a flowered dress.

"Do you have to work here all day?" said Thom. "Will's going to help me with the cream puffs. You could help too."

"Can't. I'm still officially grounded."

"What exactly did you do?" said Will.

"I used Peaches' clothesline to make a tightrope from the corner of our roof to the shed. Dad said I could have broken my neck!"

Will thought Emma was the most daring girl he had ever met. "What about the poetry reading?" he said.

"Don't worry. I'm allowed to go."

Will and Thom left then, squeezing past customers. When they got back to Thom's, Will weighed flour and cracked eggs while Thom dropped bits of butter into a pot of boiling water and stirred.

This time, while the cream puffs were baking, they both stayed glued to the glass window in the oven. "They're getting bigger," said Will.

"And golden," said Thom.

Emma arrived, breathless, when they were just about done. "Lukas took over for me and I snuck away. I figured you'd need my special touch." She peered over their shoulders. "Hey! They look perfect!"

"They *are* perfect," declared Thom a few minutes later, while they cooled on racks.

But when he cut into one with a knife, he cried, "SOGGY! They're SOGGY!"

"You were supposed to puncture them to let out the steam," said Emma, checking *Mastering the Art of French Cooking*.

"It's too late!" wailed Thom. He sank down on a chair and buried his head in his arms. "I'm not going to the poetry reading."

"You have to," said Will.

"No I don't! I'm staying right here until it's over. Go away and leave me alone!"

Emma flipped pages in the cookbook. "What does *Reine de Saba* mean?"

"I don't know," mumbled Thom. "And I don't care."

Wait a sec." Emma ran into the living room and then

came back. "Your dad says it means Queen of Sheba. We'll make a Queen of Sheba cake for the poetry reading!"

Emma shouted out ingredients. "Butter, eggs, flour, sugar, baking chocolate!" Will opened cupboards and drawers and hunted.

Thom said nothing, his face still buried.

In a few minutes, Will and Emma were weighing and mixing and stirring. "Almond extract," said Emma. "Do you have almond extract, Thom?"

Thom groaned.

"We'll use...let's see. We'll use grape jelly instead." .

Thom bolted upright. "NO! You can't just change ingredients like that! Grape jelly isn't *anything* like almond extract!"

He jumped to his feet and produced the almond extract from a cupboard above the fridge. He grabbed the mixing spoon from Emma and said, "That's not how you cream butter and sugar! I'm going to have to start all over again! You'll have to go! Get out of my kitchen! I can't concentrate!"

They left Thom poring over the recipe, muttering, "Four ounces of melted semi-sweet chocolate..."

When they got outside, Will said, "See you tonight at Vespera's poetry reading."

He headed up Black Penny Road. When he got to the castle, he had a tremendous shock.

chapter twenty-five

THE SECRET PASSAGE

A NEW SIGN HAD been nailed over the SOLD sign on the oak tree.

FOR SALE BY OWNER
INQUIRE WITHIN

So that's what Aunt Mauve meant when she said the sooner they were out, the better! He *couldn't* leave Sparrowhawk, not now. So many mysterious things had happened and the answer to them was somewhere inside the castle.

Will stormed through the door and marched directly to the Red Chamber. He found Aunt Mauve in bed under the crimson canopy, surrounded by a sea of tissues.

"You can't sell the castle!" shouted Will.

"Ah-ah-choo!" sneezed Aunt Mauve.

Will leapt back.

"I'll do what I please!" snapped Aunt Mauve. "Now go away and tell Mrs. Cherry I want my dinner in bed."

"Forget it! I'm busy."

Will shot out of the room and ran back to his tower. He lay on the four-poster bed and stared miserably into space. He had a sudden very creepy thought. *Maybe*

Hannah had died in this very bed.

His eyes flickered to the ornate twisted posts at the foot of the bed. The right post was made of some kind of dark wood; the left was lighter and the swirls in the wood went up and down instead of sideways. What about the other posts? He turned to look at the head of the bed, and a tingle went through him. They were dark wood too. Why was one post different?

He stood up on the bed, grasped the light-coloured post and twisted it. Nothing. A harder twist and the top of the post popped off, revealing a space inside. His heart pounding, he pulled out a folded piece of paper and opened it. Someone had printed *The hungry sparrowhawk guards the secret.*

Did Hannah Linley write the note? *The hungry sparrowhawk.* What did that mean? What secret?

Will ran his eyes along the frieze of stone sparrow hawks. They all looked exactly the same. He slowly studied them, one by one, comparing. That one next to the window. Was its beak slightly open?

He jumped off the bed and dragged it across the room until he was right underneath the bird. Then he hopped up on the bed and put his hands on the bird's face. He could make out faint lines in the stone that traced a big square with the sparrowhawk in the middle. He pushed on the bird's curved beak. Then he tried to pull it but the stone was smooth and slippery and he couldn't get a good grip. His fingers slid off.

Its beak was open just enough for Will to put his finger inside and wiggle it around. *Was that a bump?* He pressed down. To his shock, the stone moved. Just a little. He pushed down on the bump, as hard as he could. He grunted and pushed even harder, and all of a sudden, something gave way. The square of stone swung backwards with a grating sound, revealing rusty hinges, and a black hole appeared.

Will grabbed his torch and shone it into the hole. The light picked out a flight of rough stone steps that descended into the darkness. A musty smell drifted up. He stared down the stairs, stunned. He had found the secret passageway!

He hoisted himself through the hole, scraping his stomach on the rough stone, and found himself on a small stone landing. Step by step, he inched down the stairs, brushing aside the thick cobwebs. At the bottom, one brick-lined tunnel led to the right, one to the left. Will frowned. *Which way should I go?*

He picked the tunnel to the right. It seemed to go on forever, twisting and turning, so low in places that he had to bend over. He turned a few corners, climbed up four shallow steps cut out of rock and then made his way down a long slope. He tried to keep track of where he might be in the castle, but soon he was completely mixed up. Water seeped from the ceiling and cold drops splashed on his head. Something skittered past him in the dark, beady red eyes frozen in the beam of light.

The tunnel finally ended in another set of rough-cut stairs, this time going up. Will shone his light up but couldn't see the end. The stairs were uneven and very steep. He climbed carefully. The steps ended at a small wooden door with a heavy iron handle. He turned the handle and pushed the door. It refused to budge. A harder shove and it gave way.

Before him stretched an enormous room bathed in

light that streamed through the tall narrow windows. At one end was a fireplace as big as a cave, with a massive smoke-stained beam above it, and at the other end were two great wooden doors with black iron rings. Will's mouth dropped open. Huge blue and crimson and gold tapestries, bigger than the biggest carpets and glowing like stained glass windows, hung on the walls. *I'm in the keep*, he thought. This must be the great hall!

In a daze, he walked to the nearest tapestry and stared up at it. It was a scene of a hunting party woven in brilliant colours. Men in tunics, horses with handsome saddles and glittering bridles and lean greyhounds gathered in front of a big stone castle. Behind the castle was a forest filled with fantastic trees and flowers and all kinds of creatures – rabbits, frogs, a deer with silver antlers and a golden pheasant.

"It's Sparrowhawk Hall!" said Will.

But it was the words woven out of fine gold thread at the top of the tapestry that took his breath away.

The Hunt for the Griffin of Darkwood.

"The Griffin of Darkwood," Will whispered. A prickle ran up his spine. He was sure that the letters were the same as the letters on his piece of tapestry.

He ran to the next tapestry. It was a picture of a magnificent griffin, backed up against a cliff and circled by hunters with spears. The delicate gold letters at the top of the tapestry said,

The Griffin of Darkwood is Captured.

Will rushed to the last tapestry. Twelve black horses dragged the chained bloodstained griffin through the forest. Spears protruded from its bowed neck. Will read,

The Griffin of Darkwood is Taken to the Castle.

The tapestries told a story. Will paced back and forth between them. Who had woven them? Was it Morgan Moonstone? Were they magic tapestries? And where did his piece belong? If only he had brought it with him!

He studied each tapestry one more time, standing longest in front of the griffin in chains, its eyes blazing with rage and pain. The story couldn't end just like that. What had happened to the griffin after it was taken to the castle?

"There's one more tapestry," he said. "There *has* to be. And somehow I've got a piece of it."

chapter twenty-six

THE POETRY READING

)

WILL TORE HIMSELF AWAY from the tapestries and walked over to the huge wooden doors. With both hands he grasped one of the iron rings and turned it to the left. The door groaned and opened slowly toward him. On the other side was a wall of rubble and broken stone. That meant there was only one way into the great hall – through the secret passage. He turned back into the room. He wanted to gaze at the magnificent tapestries forever, but it was getting late, and there was no way he was going to miss Vespera's poetry reading. He went back through the little door, taking one last look around before he closed it.

Will edged down the steep steps, shining the torch ahead of him. Back he went, through the dark winding tunnel with its twists and turns. When he got to the steps to the tower, he shone his torch down the other passageway. Where did it go? Nothing could be as amazing as the great hall, but he would love to know. *Next time*, he promised himself, as he climbed up the steps, wiggled through the hole and dropped onto the bed.

He pressed the bump in the sparrowhawk's beak and the stone slab creaked back into place. *You would never know it was there*, he thought, *if you didn't know the secret.* He dragged the bed back to its usual place and looked around to make sure everything looked exactly the same. He stuffed Hannah's note into his jeans pocket. He had no idea if Mr. Cherry snooped in his tower but he wasn't taking any chances.

He sped out of the castle, stopping at Aunt Mauve's FOR SALE sign which was tilting to one side and tugging at it until the nails popped loose. He dragged the sign into the long grass and flew down to the bookstore.

�֎

Will slid into the empty seat beside Thom and Emma. Peaches, curled up under Emma's chair, thumped his tail. All the other seats were taken. Scattered among the tourists and villagers, Will spotted John Fairweather, Granny Storm – sitting with Star and all the Storm children – and Madeleine de Luca. Cups, saucers, a tea pot and a huge chocolate-frosted Queen of Sheba cake were laid out on a table.

"Where were you?" asked Thom. "I had to keep telling people they couldn't sit here. Did you see my cake?"

"I've got big news," said Will. "*Big* news!"

"Shhh," someone behind them said.

"I'll tell you later," Will whispered.

Favian stood at the front beside Vespera, who was seated at a small table with a copy of A *Mystical Muse* and an oil lamp on it. He had dimmed the shop lights and lit the lamp.

"Tonight I'm delighted to introduce our famous resident poet," he said. "Vespera Moonstone."

Vespera began to read in her soft musical voice. In

seconds Will had fallen under the spell of the magical poems. Vespera was a brilliant writer, and he felt so lucky that she was his friend. After each poem, the audience applauded vigorously.

It was over too soon. A flurry of book-buying and tea and cake followed.

"Magnificent, Thom," said Vespera, licking icing off her fingers. "How clever of you to think of a cake! Much more exciting than dull old cream puffs!"

Will pulled Thom and Emma into a corner.

"I found it!" he said.

"Found what?" asked Emma, her mouth full of cake.

"The secret passage. Hannah left a note in the bedpost. There's a hole behind one of the stone sparrowhawks in the tower. It goes to a tunnel. I followed it all the way to the keep."

Will's words tumbled over each other as he told them about his amazing discovery.

"I wish I'd been there!" cried Emma. "Tapestries and a griffin! It's gotta have something to do with the curse."

"That's what I think," said Will. "I'll show you tomorrow. You're not going to believe it!"

"Madeleine de Luca's staring at us," said Thom.

Emma and Will talked in whispers, making plans, but Thom was silent, his eyes dark with worry.

"You three look very secretive," said Star, coming up to them with a smile. "It's time to go now, Emma. Granny Storm's getting impatient."

John Fairweather looked exhausted and Thom said, "I better go too."

After his friends had gone, Will hung around until only a few people were left, looking at books and chatting with Vespera. He was bursting to talk to Favian about his discovery.

Favian was talking to a man in a black suit. Will caught scraps of the conversation. The man said, "This is the perfect place to hold readings...tremendous atmosphere...I could organize a series of famous authors and poets..."

When the man paused for a breath, Will said, "Favian, can I talk to you?"

Favian frowned. "Good heavens. Are you still here? I'm busy right now. It will have to wait until tomorrow."

"It's important," said Will.

But Favian turned back to the man. "I'm intrigued by the idea. We could start –"

"Favian, *please*."

It was hopeless. Favian didn't even hear him.

Will walked through the dark village to the castle. When he got back to the tower, he scrambled up on the bed and pulled himself through the trap door and onto the roof. Stars twinkled overhead and the night air was cool on his cheeks.

Suddenly a light flickered in the ruined courtyard, crisscrossing back and forth.

He watched the light bob in front of the keep. After ten minutes, the light moved back across the courtyard and disappeared.

Mr. Cherry, thought Will, his stomach tightening.

Only a pile of fallen stone separated Mr. Cherry from the magnificent tapestries in the great hall. Was he after the tapestries? Did he know about them?

Only a pile of fallen stone. Was it enough?

chapter twenty-seven

THIEVES!

)

IN THE MORNING, Will slipped his scrap of tapestry into his pocket and left the castle.

"Where are you going?" shouted Thom from his window as Will passed underneath.

"To talk to Favian."

"Wait for me!"

A *Sorry We're Closed* sign hung on the bookstore door, but Favian opened it when Will knocked and they went inside.

"There's something I have to tell you," Will burst out.

At that moment, there was another urgent knock on the door.

"Who on earth?" Favian opened the door again and stuck his head out. "I'm not open yet. I came in early to clean up from the poetry reading last night."

A woman in a charcoal suit and crisp white blouse, carrying a brown leather briefcase, stood in the doorway. "Just a few minutes of your time," she said. "It's terribly important."

With a sigh, Favian opened the door wider and ushered his visitor in.

"I'll get right to the point." She set her briefcase on the

rolltop desk. "My name is Kate Winters. I'm a private investigator. I've been driving all night. Nothing looks open, but I saw your light on. I've been trying to locate a couple called Chadwick and Charmaine Neale for four years. They're a pair of international art thieves. There's a warrant out for their arrest."

She opened the briefcase and removed a large photograph. Favian peered at it and Will and Thom sidled closer so they could see too. The photograph was of a man with glasses and a moustache and woman with long blonde hair walking down a street.

"This photograph is twelve years old. When it was taken, they were going under the aliases of Cheryl and Chauncey Turner," said Kate. "They were the housekeeper and gardener at Langton Hall. The police arrested them for stealing eighteenth century watercolours. They spent four years in Stonewall Prison."

She took out another photograph of a black-haired woman and a bearded man and slapped it down. "Charles and Christine Renshaw. Same people. They're masters of disguise. Employed as a housekeeper and chauffeur by a spinster called Esma Jameston. She collects rare hand painted music boxes."

"Let me guess," said Favian. "They stole them."

"Sentenced to fifteen years. Escaped from Stonewall in a laundry truck after serving six years. No one's seen them since."

Will stared at the photographs.

"What does this have to do with us?" asked Favian. "Have the police hired you to look for them?"

"Esma Jameston has. She wants her music boxes back. I was hot on the trail until a few weeks ago, and then it went cold. Until yesterday. Esma's nephew was here on a bus tour. He said he's positive he saw Chadwick Neale. He would have followed him but he disappeared down one of those funny little streets. Called something like Shadow Alley."

"It's the Cherrys!" said Will. "In the photographs. I saw Mrs. Cherry once without her wig, washing dishes. I thought it was a stranger with long blonde hair."

Favian took a closer look. "I believe you're right!"

"I presume Sparrowhawk Hall is a lovely old estate full of rare art," said Kate.

Favian shook his head. "Actually it's mostly a ruin. There's some ghastly family portraits and that's about all. I have no idea what the Cherrys could be after." He tore his eyes away from the photographs. "What happens now?"

Kate slid the photographs back in her briefcase and snapped it shut. "Nothing. We don't want to alert them. I'll contact the police at once."

"The nearest detachment is in Chipping," said Favian. "They won't get here until tomorrow."

"Everyone must stay away from the castle," said Kate. "The Cherrys are dangerous." She looked sternly at Thom and Will. "Do you understand that?"

The boys looked at each other and nodded.

Will waited until Kate had left. "The castle's not just full of family portraits!" he said. "There's three huge tapestries! They're in the great hall."

Favian stared at him. "Tell me everything. No, wait a minute. Vespera will want to hear this too."

He used the phone behind his desk and in ten minutes Vespera appeared, her frizzy hair blown every which way and her cheeks rosy. "There's going to be a storm," she said. "Thunderclouds are building up over the hills. Now what's this all about, Favian?"

Favian filled Vespera in on Kate Winter's visit. "So the Cherrys are crooks!" she said. "I never liked the look of them!"

"And now your turn, Will," said Favian.

Will poured out his story. "The tapestries are amazing," he finished. "You've got to see them!"

"To think of you in that secret passageway," said Vespera. "You're giving me goosebumps."

"You're a brave young man," said Favian.

"There's gotta be a fourth tapestry," said Will. "They tell a story, but the story's not finished."

"But a fourth tapestry," said Favian. "If there was one, why wouldn't it be there with the others?"

"I don't know," said Will, "but I know it existed. I've got a piece of it." He took the scrap of tapestry out of his pocket.

"How on earth did you get it?" asked Favian.

"It was with a picture of my grandfather Sterling Moonstone," said Will.

"Your grandfather was Sterling?" said Vespera.

"We just found out," said Favian.

"Do you think that Morgan Moonstone wove the tapestries?" said Will.

"What an astounding idea!" said Favian.

"That would mean that they're magic!" said Will. "It's because of Hannah I found the tapestries. No one's ever told me what really happened to her."

"She disappeared," said Vespera. "She was missing for a day and a night. Lord and Lady Linley were frantic. She was found wandering in the forest near the castle. She was delirious. She babbled on about a secret passage and tapestries. We always thought there was more, something she wasn't telling us. She was so very ill."

Vespera squeezed Favian's hand. "We were best friends, you see, the four of us. Favian, myself, Sterling and Hannah."

"And then what happened?" said Thom.

Vespera said softly, "Hannah slipped into a coma and died. Shortly after that Lord Linley boarded up the castle and he and Lady Linley moved far away. That was over forty years ago. We were all so surprised to hear that the castle was for sale."

"Do you think Hannah saw the same tapestries that Will saw?" asked Thom.

"Yes," said Vespera. "And somehow she ended up in the forest, lost and desperately ill."

"Now what happens?" asked Will. "The Cherrys are after the tapestries. I know it!"

"Once the Cherrys have been arrested, I'll arrange a bulldozer to move that rubble blocking the front doors to the great hall," said Favian. "The tapestries are national treasures. They should be preserved. And in the meantime, we'll just have to wait for the police."

"I pray they're not too late," said Vespera.

"Let's go tell Emma," said Thom.

"Just remember what Kate said," Favian cautioned. "Stay away from the castle."

Thom shivered. "I never want to see the castle again."

"That's fine for you to say, Thom, but I live there," said Will.

"You can stay with me or Vespera tonight, Will,"

Favian said.

Will and Thom left the shop.

"What if Mr. Cherry goes into the tower and finds the secret passageway?" asked Thom.

"I moved the stone back," Will told him. "If you didn't know it was there, you'd never see it. I only found it because of Hannah's note."

He clamped his hand over his pocket. "Hannah's note! It's gone. I must have dropped it somewhere." He groaned. "What if the Cherrys find it?"

Thom's eyes widened.

"I have to go back," said Will.

"You can't. Kate said the Cherrys were dangerous. We promised not to go to the castle."

"We never promised anything," said Will. "I have no choice."

Thom's face turned white. "Then I'm coming with you."

chapter twenty-eight

TRAPPED

🌙

WILL AND THOM RACED across the courtyard. Ominous black clouds darkened the sky, making it feel like evening. They met Emma and Peaches outside *The Winking Cat*.

"I've been looking everywhere for you!" said Emma.

"We're going to the castle!" said Will. "The Cherrys are trying to steal the tapestries.

They quickly filled Emma in.

"I'm coming too," said Emma. "Safety in numbers"

When they got back to the castle, the pink van was parked in its usual spot in the weeds. Were the tapestries inside? Had the Cherrys somehow managed to drag them through the secret passageway? They tried to peer through the windows, but the glass had been smeared with mud and they couldn't see anything.

"We need to sabotage the van," said Emma.

"Nails," suggested Thom. "We could stick them in the tires."

Will remembered seeing a rusty can of nails in the old shed. He ran and got them, and he and Emma jabbed them into the tires while Thom acted as the lookout.

Will's heart thudded as they climbed the spiral stairs to his tower. There was no sign of the note. Was that a faint smell of garlic?

He wouldn't relax until he saw that the tapestries were safe on the walls of the great hall. "We're going in!" he said. "Help me move the bed."

When the bed was under the stone sparrowhawk, Will said, "Watch this!" He climbed onto the bed and pushed the bump in the sparrowhawk's beak. The stone slab swung backwards.

"Wow!" said Emma.

Thom's eyes popped wide open. One by one they climbed through the hole in the wall. "*Hooo-whooo-hooo,*" howled Peaches from the middle of the bed. Emma leaned down and hoisted him up, his paws scrabbling on the stone wall. She dragged him through the hole and he followed them down the steep cobwebby staircase.

Will shone the torch ahead into the gloom. When they got to the bottom, he said, "We're going this way."

"Where does that go?" said Emma, pointing up the other tunnel.

"Don't know."

No one spoke as they walked along the narrow passage, ducking their heads at the low places. They went up the four steps cut out of the rock and down the long slope.

"We're under the ruins now," said Will. "We're coming to the keep."

Two more corners and his torch beamed onto the rough steep steps set into the stone wall. They climbed up slowly. Will opened the door at the top, and one by one they scrambled into the enormous room.

Daylight from the narrow windows shone on the great tapestries. Will's shoulders sagged with relief. "They're still here."

"They're huge!" said Emma.

"They're beautiful," breathed Thom.

Will stood in front of the first tapestry. He took out his scrap of material and held it up, comparing the writing. The letters were exactly the same. "Look at this!" he cried. "I was right. There is one more tapestry! And this is a piece from it."

Questions tumbled about in Will's head. Had Morgan Moonstone woven it? What did it say? Where was it? And how had he ended up with a piece?

Boom! There was a loud rumble deep inside the castle and the sound of crashing rock.

Boom!

"What's happening?" yelled Thom.

Boom!

Emma screamed. "It's an earthquake!"

"We gotta get back," cried Will. "Come on!"

"*Hooo-whooo-hooo*," howled Peaches as they fled through the door onto the stairs. On the third step from the bottom, Will tripped. He shone the torch on his feet. Chunks of stone were scattered across the rest of the stairs.

Thom and Emma crowded behind him.

"The roof's caving in!" said Emma.

They climbed over the stones and hurried along the tunnel, stumbling over broken bricks and more stones. Was the whole castle going to collapse?

When they got to the tower stairs, Will, his heart pounding, stared in horror. A mass of rubble filled the staircase. There was no way they could go up.

"We're going to be buried alive!" cried Thom. "I knew we shouldn't have come. I knew it!"

"No we aren't," said Will. "We'll find a way out of here." He turned around and shone the torch up the other tunnel. "We'll go this way. It's gotta go somewhere."

Sweat slickened Will's neck and a feeling of dread slipped over him. He had got his friends into this mess. If they didn't turn up sooner or later, would Favian guess that they had gone back into the secret passage? How would he ever find them?

They followed the turns and twists of the passage, tripping over fallen bricks.

The walls changed from brick to rough stone. The passage grew narrower and narrower and the ceiling lowered until they had to bend over. They were close to the end, Will guessed, but what would they find?

Then he cried out, "I see daylight! And I can hear something. I think it's the wind!"

He stopped with a jolt of shock. They had come to a small rocky ledge, somewhere just below the guard's walk, where Mr. Cherry had threatened him that first day. There was a long sheer drop down the castle wall and then down the rugged face of the cliff to the black river far below.

"Hey! Look out!" said Will, as Thom and Emma bumped up against him. "Don't let Peaches push me!"

The ledge was slick with water and very slippery.

_Ke-ke-ke-ke!_ A sparrowhawk was riding the wind, a limp brown body dangling from its beak. It swooped in close to the castle wall, and Will put his arms up to protect himself. _Ke-ke-ke_ it shrieked, fighting the wind with powerful flaps of its wings.

"_RUFF! RUFF!_" barked Peaches.

"Get back!" cried Thom, grabbing Will's arm. "You'll

be blown right off!"

"Wait a sec," said Will. "And hang on to Peaches!" He lay on his stomach and inched forward. He peered over the ledge. "There's steps! Hundreds of them," he shouted so he could be heard over the screaming wind. "Cut into the wall. They look like they go right down to the river."

"No way," moaned Thom. "There's no way I'm going! We'll fall and be killed! We'll drown!"

Will felt dizzy. "We'd need a boat anyway," he said. He slid back until he was inside the passage with the others.

"Now what?" said Emma, gripping Peaches' collar.

"We'll go back," said Will. "We'll just have to try to move those rocks."

On the way back, no one spoke.

"I'm going to turn the torch off, just for a little while, to save the batteries," said Will. But the darkness was so awful that Thom gave a cry and even Emma gasped, so he hastily flicked the light back on.

"Peaches is gone!" said Emma suddenly. "He was right behind me but he's gone now!"

"Why did you let go of his collar?" said Thom. "Peaches! Peaches! Come on back, boy."

"Peaches!" yelled Will. "Peaches, where are you?"

And then the dog seemed to pop right out of the wall by their feet.

"Hey! Where did you come from?" asked Emma. "Shine your light down here, Will."

Will shone the beam of light on the wall, revealing a small opening, close to the ground. He crouched down. "It's a tunnel," he said. "We must have walked right past it before!"

"Peaches found it," said Emma. "Good boy, Peaches! Good boy!"

"We're not going in there, are we?" said Thom.

"We have to," said Will. "Come on!"

They crawled in on their hands and knees, Will leading the way. The tunnel was cut out of the rock and had a hard-packed dirt floor with jagged walls that scraped their arms. Icy water dripped down on them.

The tunnel seemed to go on forever. And then Will felt cool air on his face and he smelled a rich earthy scent.

"We're at the end!" he shouted.

chapter twenty-nine

IN THE FOREST

WILL SQUEEZED UNDER an overhanging ledge of rock and stood up. Emma and Thom crawled out beside him.

Tall skinny trees with black trunks surrounded them. Straggly grey moss dangled in long wispy strands from the branches. Vines swarmed like snakes over fallen logs and rotten stumps.

"This is the forest!" said Thom. "We're not supposed to be in here!"

"The curse!" said Emma.

"*Hoo-whoo-hooo,*" howled Peaches.

An opening in the dark trees looked like a trail. They started walking, scrambling over logs and ducking under low-hanging branches. Dead wood snapped under their feet and vines grabbed at their clothes. The only living creature they passed was a fat white spider in a silver cobweb, suspended like lace between two trees.

Emma bent down beside a cluster of scarlet toadstools.

"Don't touch those!" said Will. "They're probably poisonous!"

"I wasn't going to," said Emma.

The trail was getting harder to find. Will pushed branches out of his face.

"Will, slow down," said Emma. "We have to wait for Thom."

Will looked back. Thom and Peaches were lagging behind. Thom groaned and sank down on a log. He hung his head and stared at the ground and Peaches licked his hand.

Will and Emma hurried back. Thom lifted his head. His white face shone with sweat. "I'm sorry. I...I can't go on. There's...there's something terrible happening here."

"We gotta keep going," said Will.

Thom groaned again and staggered to his feet. He stumbled behind the others like an old man.

Will glimpsed a pale green light through the trees. "There's something up ahead. I'm not sure what it is."

He squeezed between the black trunks of two trees and stepped into a clearing. In the middle was a thick wooden pole with a long rusty chain dangling from the top.

"This is it," said Thom. "This is where it's coming from. Something suffered here. It's choking me. I can't breathe."

"Something was chained up here," said Emma.

"It must have paced around and around," said Will, looking at the deep rut that circled the pole.

"It looks like the chain's been broken," said Emma. "What kind of creature could break a thick chain like that?"

"I can't stay here,' whispered Thom. "Please."

Suddenly Will saw a movement out of the corner of his eye, an enormous shadow shifting behind the dark trees. The hackles on Peaches' back rose, and a low growl rumbled in his throat.

"What is it?" cried Emma.

Will's heart pounded in his ears. Something was watching them. "Over there!" he shouted.

They all stared into the trees.

"Let's –" Emma started to say but her words turned into a scream. Two huge wings swept through the air, smashing branches, almost knocking them down with a blast of wind. A long tawny tail lashed back and forth.

"Look out!" yelled Emma.

Will stared into a pair of blazing eyes. A tremendous shriek filled the forest. His legs went weak and his throat dry. He fell backwards, shielding his face with his hands. There was a sudden throbbing in his pocket. Will reached in and pulled out the piece of tapestry. The letters glowed as if they were made out of molten gold.

He held the piece of tapestry high above him. There was a tremendous gust of wind and everything swirled around him. The last thing he heard was Thom screaming.

chapter thirty

WHERE IS THOM?

$$\smile$$

WILL SNAPPED OPEN his eyes. He was standing beside
Emma and Peaches, his fingers gripping the tapestry
scrap, his knuckles white. The stone creature stared down
at them from the archway on the castle.

"What happened?" said Emma shakily.

Will struggled to make sense of everything. "My piece
of tapestry...it saved us...it brought us here."

"A griffin!" said Emma. "I saw it!"

Will sucked in his breath. So it wasn't just him! Emma
had seen it too. It was a griffin! He looked around in a
panic. Wind and rain lashed at their faces. Where was
Thom?

"Thom!" shouted Will. "Thom, where are you?"

"Thom!" yelled Emma. "Thom!"

The storm raged around them. The wind snatched
Thom's name and tossed it back in their faces. Will barely
understood what had happened. The scrap of tapestry had
transported them out of that terrible forest and away from
the griffin. They were safe, but had Thom been left
behind?

Lightning flashed and thunder cracked. The freezing
rain plastered Emma's and Will's clothes to their backs.

Peaches whined and pushed himself between Emma's legs.

Emma slipped her hand into Will's.

They hollered for Thom until their voices were hoarse. It was hopeless. They could barely hear themselves over the screaming wind.

Crack. The huge oak tree near the castle smashed to the ground.

"We need help!" said Emma.

Their hands broke apart and they raced down Black Penny Road. *It can't be later than noon,* Will thought, *but it's as dark as night.* Water streamed in rivers through the cobblestones. Shutters were fastened tight and most of the shops were closed. Candlelight flickered in a few windows.

"The power must be out," said Emma.

They ran all the way to the Fairweather's flat. John Fairweather was reading by candlelight.

"The earthquake," he said. "I've been so worried about you. There's damage in the village."

His face turned ashen as Will and Emma poured out their story. "My son!" he said. He picked up the phone, exclaiming, "Thank God it still works!"

A search party assembled quickly. Men and women in rain slickers and boots gathered in the flat. Favian came and Emma's father, Peter Storm, with a bag of dry clothes. For the first time, John seemed to see the cold dripping children and the sodden dog. "You'll catch your death, both of you. Put on these clothes. And I'll get an old towel for Peaches."

Will changed into a pair of Lukas's jeans and a warm sweatshirt. He took the piece of tapestry out of his jacket pocket. It had saved their lives.

Favian came over. "I want to hear everything," he said

quietly. "But first we must find Thom."

Within minutes, the searchers had left. The flat was cold and empty without Thom. They settled in to wait. It was the longest afternoon Will could ever remember. John sat at the window and stared out at the glistening wet street. Will and Emma huddled on the floor, talking quietly, with Peaches curled up beside them.

The clock ticked from four to five to six o'clock. At seven o'clock, they had bowls of cornflakes. The rain rattled the windows and the wind shrieked eerily between the loose shutters. John's eyes probed the blackness for a sign that the searchers were returning.

Just after eight, a line of lights flickered in the dark street. John gave a small cry and Emma and Will ran to the window. "They wouldn't come back without him," John said. Hope and fear flashed across his face.

The door opened and the heavy-set man who owned the bakery carried Thom inside the flat. The boy lay still in his arms, his face like wax and his eyes closed.

"Thom –" John choked.

"He's cold and exhausted," said Emma's father, who had followed them in. "We found him in the forest. Favian has gone for the doctor, and he'll be here straightaway."

He looked at Emma and Will. "I'm taking you and Peaches back to the house. Will, you'll stay the night with us. Star will want to keep an eye on you. We'll let your aunt know."

Will was too tired to argue. The men had carried Thom into his bedroom, their low voices murmuring. On the way down the stairs, a man rushed up past them, carrying a black doctor's bag.

When they got to the old apple barn, the other Storm children had gone to bed. An oil lamp burned in the kitchen and Granny Storm and Star were sitting over cups of tea, heated up on a camp stove.

"Thom?" said Star.

"Safe at home," said her husband Peter. "But he's in a bad way. Too much exposure to the storm." He hesitated. "And something else is wrong too. It's as if something has paralyzed him. The doctor is with him now."

Granny's eyes glittered when she saw Will. "I warned you. I said you would need courage in the days to come. And it's not over yet. It's far from over."

A tremor ran through Will. What did she mean?

"Hannah Linley was found wandering in the forest in a storm." Granny's voice rose. "She died two days later."

"That's enough, Granny!" said Emma's father sharply. "Everyone's upset enough."

"It's the griffin's curse. It'll –"

"Enough!" roared Peter.

Granny muttered crossly into her tea, but she didn't say another word.

Star sprang up, arranging a bed and blankets for Will in the spare room. "I'm not tired," he protested as Star tucked him in. But in less than five minutes he was asleep.

He dreamed he was inside Granny Storm's crystal ball and this time, he couldn't get out.

chapter thirty-one

MORGAN MOONSTONE'S STORY

☽

SOMEONE WAS SHAKING Will's shoulder. He burrowed deeper into the warm blankets. "Will, wake up," whispered Star.

Will's eyes blinked open. "Thom –"

"There's no improvement yet. But he's a brave boy. He'll pull through. Favian Longstaff just phoned. He says you must come to the bookstore immediately."

"Now? What time is it?"

"It's ten o'clock. You've only been asleep an hour. But Favian said it was urgent."

"What –"

"No idea. Peter's going to take you. The storm hasn't eased at all. And there's something else. Favian said to bring the piece of tapestry."

Will struggled back into the clothes he had borrowed from Lukas. His jacket was still wet so Star gave him one of Lukas's heavy jackets to wear. He slipped the scrap of tapestry into the pocket.

He shivered as they went out into the wild night and down the road to the village square. The EX LIBRIS sign over the bookstore was banging back and forth in the wind. A candle burned in the window. Favian greeted them at the door.

"Any word on Thom?" Peter asked.

Favian shook his head. "Nothing. He's still unconscious. They'll take him to the hospital in Chipping as soon as it's light out." He put his hand on Will's shoulder. "I'll take care of our boy here. You get back to your family, Peter."

"Favian," Will said urgently, when Peter had left. "We found a tunnel into the forest. I think that's how Hannah got in. And we saw a griffin!"

"What a night!" cried Favian.

"It was terrible," said Will. "Thom got so sick. He said he felt this terrible suffering. It came from the griffin. Hannah must have felt it too. You said she had the same powers as Thom. I think it killed her."

"We have so much to talk about," said Favian. "Astounding things have happened since you came to Sparrowhawk. But I must show you this first."

He picked up a parcel wrapped in brown paper. "This arrived for you in this afternoon's post. With the scare over Thom, I didn't have a chance to give it to you. It's from Mr. Barnaby."

"Should I open it now?" asked Will, his voice trembling.

"I think you should open it when you're alone," said Favian. "But that is not why I sent for you on such a wicked night. I've found something. Come with me."

Favian led Will between the tall tiers of books into the depths of the shadowy shop. A purple candle burned on a round table, casting a tiny pool of light on several sheets of paper, as thin as parchment and yellowed with age.

"I found these papers hidden in one of Ebenezer Moonstone's ancient books."

Will picked up the first paper. He read out loud the words written in black ink at the top.

"An account of the events at Sparrowhawk Hall as told by Morgan Moonstone to his wife Elizabeth Moonstone in the year 1604..."

Will stopped reading and stared at Favian.
"Go on," said Favian. "Read it all and then we'll talk."
Will began again.

"My name is Morgan Moonstone, master weaver. I know that I am dying. I am too weak to hold a pen and I have asked my wife Elizabeth to write my story.

On a cold spring morning, just two weeks ago, Lord Linley's servant knocked at the door of our cottage.

'Lord Linley of Sparrowhawk Hall is planning a hunt for the griffin of Darkwood,' he said. 'He summons you to weave four magic tapestries. A griffin has been sighted and the work must be completed in ten days. You must begin at once.'

My tapestries have caused the success of many hunts. Ten days was not long enough, but I could use my magic. Still I hesitated. Lord Linley had a reputation as a cruel man.
'My master will pay you well,' said the man. 'But you must work without interruption and move into the tower at the castle until you are finished.'

I set up my loom in the tower. I worked day and night with little sleep. By the eighth day, I had completed three tapestries, The Hunt for the Griffin of Darkwood, The Griffin of Darkwood is Captured and The Griffin of Darkwood is Taken to the Castle. As each tapestry was finished, Lord Linley ordered his servants to carry it to the great hall in the keep. Each was hung on the wall, hidden under cloths in preparation for the grand unveiling."

Will's heart jumped. So it was true. The tapestries in the great hall were woven by Morgan Moonstone!

"I began work on the fourth tapestry. My fingers flew over the threads. Lord Linley was impatient. He didn't want to wait until I was finished to start the hunt. With a blare of bugles and a clatter of horses' hooves, he and his men set out. From the tower window I saw the guests for the feast arriving all afternoon, lords and ladies, beautifully dressed. I heard the men in the courtyard talking. The griffin had been captured. The hunt was a success. I admit I was proud at the part my magic tapestries had played.

They brought the griffin back to the castle at nightfall. Torches flickered in the courtyard below me. Although I strained to see, I could make out only shadows.

Lord Linley burst into my tower room. He examined the last tapestry and grunted with satisfaction at the sight of the griffin lying dead in a pool of blood. I had only a few finishing touches to weave and then the golden words at the top.

The Griffin of Darkwood is Killed

'How much longer?' he demanded.

'I will be finished at midnight,' I promised.

'We will hang the tapestry one minute after midnight,' he said. 'Covered like the others. I will slay the griffin at noon tomorrow and we will feast tomorrow night.'

Lord Linley's laugh was cruel. 'It will be a fine show for my guests. We will reveal the tapestries at the feast.'

Lord Linley left.

A sudden low moaning from outside, like that of a creature in great pain, sent me to a window. I could see nothing.

I went back to my tapestry. I had only the final word, *Killed*, to weave. The moaning came again, sending shivers down my spine.

I crept down the tower stairs. No one saw me. I entered the courtyard. I stood for a moment in darkness, and then the clouds parted, and the moon shone down.

It was my first sight of a griffin. I could barely breathe. Its great wings rested on the stones. It was wrapped in chains. It watched me come.

A kind of dizziness buckled my knees and made me gasp out loud. My throat went dry. I was spellbound; filled with both awe and wretchedness.

How could anyone kill such a magnificent creature?

How could I be a part of it?

It was almost midnight when I returned to the tower. I had to change the tapestry before it was too late. It was the only way to save the griffin. The magic was difficult, but not impossible. I remembered the powerful spells that my grandfather had taught me. I stood in front of the tapestry.

'OCUD RABA ABAR DUCO!' I cried."

"OCUD RABA ABAR DUCO!" said Will. "It's a palindrome!"

"Keep reading," urged Favian.

"The threads swirled and danced in a kaleidoscope of ruby and emerald and blue. The scene in the tapestry transformed *before my eyes. When the colours settled, I studied the new tapestry with joy.*

I was lost in my work, ready to weave the final word, Escapes. I didn't hear Lord Linley's steps on the tower stairs. 'Traitor!' he hissed.

In terror, I turned to face him. He raised his sword and seconds later my chest was on fire, blood spurting like a fountain. The pain was like nothing I have ever felt before. I slumped to the floor.

Time blurred. I dimly heard the tearing of my tapestry as Lord Linley slashed at it again and again. Pieces fell in tatters around me.

His hunting boot crashed into my ribs. His footsteps clattered down the stairs. He had left me to die.

A tremendous wind blew through the opened shutters. I saw pieces of the slashed tapestry spin in a cloud of colour and disappear through the windows into the night. I grabbed at a scrap. Words, woven in golden thread. The Griffin of Darkwood. *I thrust it inside my bloody shirt and crawled to the stairs.*

Step by step, I lowered myself down. At the bottom, I pulled myself up in the doorway and listened. From the courtyard came terrible sounds, Lord Linley's curses and the roar of the griffin. I knew that Lord Linley was going to kill it. I stumbled to the stone archway. The great doors were open and I slipped outside. With Lord Linley's curses ringing in my ears, I staggered down the hill and through the narrow streets to my cottage.

Elizabeth has brought me here, to this shepherd's hut, to hide. She brings my infant son every day to see me. I have lost all track of time. Elizabeth tells me that three days have passed since Lord Linley stabbed me and destroyed the last tapestry. *The talk in the village is all about the griffin. Lord Linley stabbed it a hundred times but it would not die. He ordered his men to take it in chains to a distant part of his estate, deep in the forest.*

What have I done? Did my spell save the griffin for a lifetime of suffering?

This morning, the ground shook and Elizabeth says that the entrance to the great hall is in ruins. My tapestries are buried.

Elizabeth has nursed my wounds, but I grow steadily weaker. It is hard to speak."

At the bottom of the paper in shaky handwriting were the words:

Morgan Moonstone passed away this night, May 13, in the year of our Lord 1604.

"The griffin's still alive," said Will. "It's in the forest."

"Lord Linley couldn't kill it," said Favian. "It must be because the fourth tapestry was never completed."

"The story wasn't finished," said Will. "We found the place where the griffin was chained up. It must have broken loose. But it still couldn't escape."

"When Morgan Moonstone cast his spell to change the tapestry it went terribly wrong," said Favian. "He saved the griffin's life, but he made it a prisoner." His face paled. "First Hannah took on the griffin's suffering. It killed her. And now, Thom."

Something tugged at Will's thoughts. He scanned the ancient papers again. Words jumped out at him. *Elizabeth tells me that three days have passed since Lord Linley stabbed me and destroyed the last tapestry...Morgan Moonstone passed away this night, May 13, in the year of our Lord 1604.*

"Favian!" he said. "The fourth tapestry was destroyed at midnight on May 10. That's today. It's May 10!"

Favian held his head in his hands and groaned, "We must make sense of this!"

Will took the piece of tapestry out of his pocket. "Why do I have it?" he asked desperately. "What does it mean?"

"That scrap of tapestry has been passed down to you through generations of Moonstones," said Favian. "You have been chosen for a reason. What is it you do best, Will?"

"I don't know what you mean."

"Think, Will. Think hard. What is your gift?"

Will thought about Emma saying that everyone had a passion. "I used to write," he said slowly.

"Then that is what you must do! Remember, a tapestry tells a story. You must write the story of the fourth tapestry and set the griffin free. It's our only chance to save Thom."

"But I can't. I can't write any more...I CAN'T! I don't know how...my mother..."

Will's throat closed and his eyes filled with tears.

"It's the only way," insisted Favian. "You must write it in the tower. The magic will be strongest there."

Just then, the grandfather clock in the corner of the bookstore struck eleven hours.

"One hour until midnight," said Favian. "Go now. There is still time."

chapter thirty-two

A MAGIC PENCIL

WILL RACED UP Black Penny Road, clutching the parcel from Mr. Barnaby. The wind had stopped. The silence that hung over the winding cobblestone streets was worse than the storm. Puddles gleamed like black oil in the lamplight and a cat's luminous eyes shone behind a dark window. The shutters at Thom's flat were fastened tight.

The castle was in shadow, a sleeping giant hidden in the dark. Will almost bumped into the pink van, which was parked in front of the stone entranceway. The heavy castle door creaked open and a light blinded his eyes.

"You!" a voice spat.

Mr. Cherry! The light was so bright that Will couldn't see Mr. Cherry's face. Will darted sideways, but Mr. Cherry grabbed his arm and swung him around.

"Let me go!" yelled Will.

"You picked an unfortunate time to come home," hissed Mr. Cherry. "Very unfortunate." He gripped Will tighter and dragged him into the castle.

Will fought hard, struggling to free himself, clutching the parcel to his chest.

"If there's one thing I despise, it's a meddling boy!" said Mr. Cherry.

"I know all about you!" said Will. He wriggled and twisted, but he couldn't break away. "You're a thief! You're after the tapestries, but you'll never find them!"

Mr. Cherry barked with laughter. "Too late. That convenient little earthquake opened up the keep. It's still a bit of a scramble between the rocks and rubble, but it's uncovered the front entrance. There's plenty of room to bring the tapestries out."

"The police are coming!" Will lied desperately. They're at the bookstore now. I've just come from there!"

Mr. Cherry cursed. Will wrenched his arm free and ran through the doorway to the tower stairs. He slammed the door behind him and doubled over, trying to catch his breath. Mr. Cherry cursed again and Will heard the clank of a key turning in the wooden door. Mr. Cherry's horrible laugh drifted through the door. It sent shivers up and down Will's spine.

"Don't think your wretched aunt will let you out," the man snarled. "I've locked her in too!"

"The police are coming!" shouted Will. His words were met with silence. Was Mr. Cherry still standing behind the wooden door?

He stumbled up the spiral stairs. The long red candles were burning, as tall as the day he bought them. He sat on the bed and looked at the parcel. It was addressed to *Master William Poppy c/o Ex Libris Bookstore, Sparrowhawk*. In the top left corner it said *Barnaby Book Publishers Inc.* Will was afraid to open it.

He forced himself to tear off the paper. It was a book, with a handsome blue cover. The words *The Magical Night* were emblazoned across the top in gold letters and the author's name *Adrienna Poppy* stood out boldly at the bottom.

Will opened the cover and the words jumped out at him.

For William, a writer.

He swallowed. He wasn't a writer, not any more. Maybe he never had been. The task Favian had set him was impossible. How could he write the griffin's story?

There was a folded piece of paper tucked inside the book. He took it out and read it.

Dear William,

I promised your mother that you would have the first copy of her book.

I have just returned from a world tour promoting The Magical Night. *My predictions of a runaway best-seller have come true! Tell Favian Longstaff that I will personally deliver his order of one hundred books on Wednesday. I am looking forward to seeing you.*

Your friend,

Mr. Barnaby

P.S. I am sending this to the bookstore. I believe it is safer that way. Your comment "What happened to the money?" has concerned me. We will discuss it when I arrive.

Wednesday, thought Will. *That is tomorrow.*

Angry voices erupted outside the tower window. With heavy legs Will went to the window to look. Mr. Cherry was hollering at a woman with long blonde hair. She turned her head. It was Mrs. Cherry!

"There's no time! The police are coming!" shouted Mr. Cherry.

They got inside the van and roared down the road, vanishing into the night.

Did they have the tapestries? Would the nails stuck in the tires work? Will groaned. He had no idea.

And now he was locked in the tower with no way to get out.

He paced back and forth. He took one more look out the window. The Muses stood below the tower, looking up at him. He felt sick. How much time did he have left until midnight? He looked at his watch. Thirty minutes.

"YOU DON'T UNDERSTAND!" he shouted to the Muses. "I CAN'T write!"

He pulled away from the window and at that moment, the pencil box began to glow. He opened it and took out the photograph of his grandparents and Adrienna. And then he had a tremendous shock. In the bottom of the box was a slender purple pencil covered with sparkling stars.

He could hear his mother's gentle voice. "These are my magic pencils, William. One hundred pencils, one for each chapter."

But now there was one more. Where had it come from? He picked it up and something tremendous happened. He felt his mother holding his hand.

His heart beating faster, Will opened his trunk and took out the writing book with the emerald cover, the book that he had been saving. He cleared a space at the table and sat down on the chair. He put the piece of tapestry on the table in front of him. Then he picked up the magic pencil and began to write.

chapter thirty-three

A MAGICAL NIGHT

)

The Griffin of Darkwood Escapes
Once upon a time, there was a griffin and a boy who was a Moonstone...
Outside the castle tower, a fox barked in the forest. Granny Storm's sparrowhawk, Prospero, swooped low across the sky, searching for its dinner. Macavity trotted down Lantern Lane, his eyes changing from purple to green. Two people in the sleeping village were awake; John Fairweather, sitting beside Thom's bed, and Favian, pacing back and forth in the bookstore.

Inside the castle tower, the red candles burned and Will wrote and wrote.

The trees swayed back and forth and the griffin flew up out of the forest. Its eyes blazed with triumph. The boy stood at the tower window, watching. He knew it was his powerful magic that had saved the griffin. The griffin let out a tremendous shriek. It soared into the night sky...
Will continued pouring his story into the book. The clock tower in the village struck twelve times. Will wrote

The End

It wasn't exactly a novel, but he had finished it. Will felt drained, like he had just run a marathon. The flames on the tall red candles spluttered. He jumped on the bed and opened the door to the tower roof. He pulled himself up. Moonlight flooded the sky and shimmered on the roofs of the village below and the dark forest. Everything was holding its breath.

"I did it!" shouted Will.

A sudden movement caught his eye. A circle of trees in the middle of the still forest thrashed from side to side as if they were being battered in a terrible storm. He stared in astonishment. Trunks cracked and snapped, and branches flew into the air.

A piercing screech sent shivers up his spine. A huge creature rose out of the forest and flew toward the tower. The griffin!

Massive wings beat the air. They were so huge that they made their own wind, a wind that swirled around the tower and almost knocked Will over.

"It's going to land here!" he cried, leaping back.

The griffin hovered above him, its talons extended. Its immense wings blocked the moonlight and its dark shadow fell on Will. He crouched, his heart pounding wildly. The griffin landed beside him, its claws scrabbling on the stone roof. It folded its wings back.

The creature tilted its head and gazed at Will, its eyes shining with triumph.

Will stood up slowly. The griffin lowered its belly until its broad tawny back was level with his chest. What did it want?

"*Go, William. Go now,*" whispered Adrienna Poppy.

Will wrapped his arms around the griffin's neck,

burying his fingers in the snowy feathers. He pulled himself onto its back and closed his eyes tightly. Together they soared into the night sky.

❅

Will opened his eyes. He was terrified to look down in case he got dizzy. He gripped harder and sucked in a big gulp of air, taking one quick peek back at the tower. A warm feeling of strength flowed through his arms and legs and he knew he was safe.

The griffin's cry woke the village. As it circled in the sky, people stumbled from their warm beds and into the night. They poured down the streets and filled the town square. Madeleine de Luca was there in a long black dress and so were Favian and Vespera, her beads and gypsy dress swirling in the wind, Macavity at her feet.

John Fairweather and Thom were leaning out their window. The griffin swooped lower, and Thom waved and shouted, "I'm better now! I'm better!"

The griffin circled again. All the Storms stood outside the apple barn, Granny Storm cackling with delight.

"RUFF RUFF RUFF," barked Peaches.

Then the griffin left the village and glided over the valley. The wind blew through Will's hair. He saw farmers and their families, standing in their fields, faces upturned to the sky.

Suddenly the night sky lit up in a kind of fireworks unlike anything he had seen before. Huge purple, yellow and green stars exploded before his eyes. Golden letters blazed overhead.

The Griffin of Darkwood Escapes.

Will and the griffin soared toward the distant rim of mountains. The griffin's belly skimmed the jagged peaks, white with snow. Will hung on tightly, his eyes wide with wonder.

�֍

Will saw sights that night beyond his imagination– a river that flowed with all the colours of the rainbow; two stags with silver antlers, battling on a grassy hilltop; a herd of unicorns, grazing in a meadow beside a pond filled with stars; a knight on a black horse, galloping along a silver road on a quest, the moonlight gleaming on his shield.

The sky lightened, and the sun peeked over the horizon and shone on a magnificent palace with turrets and domes. The snow on the mountain peaks turned into molten gold as the griffin turned and brought Will home.

The Griffin of Darkwood landed softly at the edge of the forest beside the castle. Will slid from its back. The griffin bowed its head and he stroked its sleek feathers. Then the creature ruffled its wings and a ripple ran through its neck and shoulders. Will stepped back and looked into its dark eyes. "You're free," he said.

He watched, thrilled, as the griffin lifted itself with its great wings into the sky. It made one last circle above him and then soared away.

Exhausted, Will collapsed on the ground under a tree and fell fast asleep.

chapter thirty-four

THE FOURTH TAPESTRY

)

BEEP! BEEP!

A car horn woke Will up. For a second, he didn't remember where he was. Then the glorious night came back to him. A thrill ran down his spine.

Beep Beep!

He scrambled to his feet and watched a black car fly up the road. A man with a crown of fluffy white hair was at the wheel. Favian sat beside him.

Mr. Barnaby!

He raced to greet them.

Mr. Barnaby and Favian stepped out of the car. Mr. Barnaby clasped Will's hand and shook it vigorously. "My dear boy! Favian has filled me in on what has been happening. If I had only known sooner!"

Will took a big breath. "Is Thom –"

"I just spoke to John Fairweather," said Favian. "Thom is fine. He's weak, but he's eating a peanut butter sandwich."

"I'll go and see him today," said Will.

"A boy flying on a griffin! It's a sight I wish I'd been here to see," said Mr. Barnaby.

"Did you bring the books?" said Will.

"One hundred copies." Mr. Barnaby beamed. "Delivered to EX LIBRIS in perfect condition!"

"They'll sell like hotcakes," Favian predicted.

"Now I must see this tower," said Mr. Barnaby. He put his hand on Will's shoulder. "Adrienna would have been proud of you."

The key to the tower door was still in the lock. Both men shuddered when Will told them how Mr. Cherry had locked him in. "The Cherrys got away," he sighed.

"Were they driving a pink van?" said Mr. Barnaby.

"Yes!"

"Then you can put your mind at rest. I passed a pink van on the road just a few miles from the village. All the tires were flat. It was surrounded by police cars with flashing lights and sirens blaring."

"So they were stopped," said Favian. That's a great relief."

"Did they have the tapestries with them?" said Will.

"I have no idea," said Mr. Barnaby.

As they climbed the tower stairs, Mr. Barnaby said, "Now where is that aunt of yours?"

"She's locked in her room!" said Will.

"We'll let her stew in her own juices a while longer," said Mr. Barnaby.

Mr. Barnaby was impressed by the tower but he said he would leave scrambling through trap doors to young boys. "I'll take your word for it that the view is splendid up there," he said. "And now we have some business to discuss." He went out to the car and returned with a briefcase, looking very important.

Will suggested the long table in the dining room for their meeting. Mr. Barnaby spread papers everywhere and talked a lot about royalties and record sales and foreign rights. Will let this sink in for a moment. Then he said, "What about Sparrowhawk Hall?"

"You own it," said Mr. Barnaby. "I realized what had happened as soon as I got your letter. Your miserable aunt has been stealing your money. She used it to buy the castle! I blame myself for not depositing it directly in your trust account."

"That's okay," said Will. He was too overjoyed to mind about anything. The castle was his! He was going to stay in Sparrowhawk with Emma and Thom.

He remembered the feeling when Emma slid her hand into his and he felt himself flush. It was something he wanted to think about more when he had time.

"And now we must attend to your aunt," said Mr. Barnaby.

"Do we have to let her out?"

"Unfortunately, we do."

Will found the big brass ring of keys in the little room that had belonged to the Cherrys. They took a while to unearth as everything was topsy-turvy – drawers pulled out, chairs tipped over. It was easy to see the Cherrys had left in a panic.

There were at least a hundred keys on the ring. Aunt Mauve shouted insults from inside the room while Will tried each key. On the ninety-sixth try, he was successful.

Aunt Mauve became more subdued when she sat at one end of the long dining-room table and faced Mr. Barnaby's stern face.

"You should be ashamed of yourself!" began Mr. Barnaby.

"But...I...er...in my defense..."

"There is no defense!" thundered Mr. Barnaby. Will looked at him admiringly. He had no idea Mr. Barnaby had it in him.

Aunt Mauve turned pale.

"I think the best thing is to send you far away," said Mr. Barnaby. "I've bought you tickets on a cruise. You must be ready to leave Sparrowhawk on this afternoon's bus."

Aunt Mauve's eyes popped open wide with delight. But after she had scurried off to pack, Mr. Barnaby winked at Will and Favian. "The cruise leaves for Antarctica in three days. The last time I checked, it was thirty degrees below zero!"

"Serves her right!" said Will. "Will I be able to stay in the castle by myself?"

"No," said Mr. Barnaby. "Absolutely not. But I thought I might move in with you. Because of your mother's book, my business has expanded. I'll be needing lots of space."

"There's seventy-three rooms!" said Will with a grin.

"One of the first things we'll do," said Favian, "is get rid of that GO AWAY on the door once and for all. Everyone wants you to stay now, Will."

"There's one thing I still don't get," said Will. "How did the Cherrys know about the tapestries?"

"Purvis Sneed," said Favian. "He was a member of the search party that looked for Hannah Linley forty-five years ago. He was a gardener here at the castle. When they carried Hannah back to the castle, she was babbling about the tapestries and the secret passage. Purvis must have heard her."

"But how did he know the Cherrys?" asked Will.

"Something rang a bell when that detective Kate Winters said the Cherrys escaped from Stonewall Prison," said Favian. "Purvis Sneed spent some years in that prison for robbery. That's where they must have met."

"What will happen to them?"

"The Cherrys will be going back to prison for a long time. But I don't imagine Purvis Sneed can be arrested for simply passing on information."

Mr. Barnaby rifled through the papers on the table. In all the excitement, Will had forgotten about the tapestries. But now he said, "I need to see if the tapestries are still here. I'd like to go by myself."

"Of course," said Favian and Mr. Barnaby nodded.

Mr. Cherry had said that the earthquake had opened up the entrance to the keep. Will ran down a passageway that led to the courtyard. He raced across the courtyard and spotted a narrow opening where the rubble piled in front of the keep had shifted. He scrambled through the opening and came to two massive wooden doors that stood partly open.

He squeezed through the opening into the great hall. The three tapestries hung in their places! His heart beat faster. On the far wall, a fourth tapestry hung, sunlight from one of the narrow windows slanting across it. Trembling, he walked up to it.

The tapestry showed a magnificent griffin with a boy clinging to its back, soaring across a night sky that exploded with colour.

"The Griffin of Darkwood Escapes," read Will. But that wasn't what made his heart race. More words were woven around the edges of the tapestry – hundreds of words, the words he had written, transformed into gold thread as delicate as spiderwebs.

"Once upon a time there was a griffin and a boy who was a Moonstone..."

Will read every word.

"The End," he said triumphantly.

And then he heard his mother, Adrienna Poppy, one last time.

"Towers and magic. Anything can happen in a castle like this, William Poppy. Anything."

Acknowledgements

I would like to thank everyone at Coteau Books who worked so hard on this story, particularly my editor Kathryn Cole.

My daughter Meghan inspired me to write a fantasy. My sister Janet read many many drafts and her suggestions were invaluable. And as always, I would like to thank my husband Larry who gives me the time to write.

BECKY CITRA is the author of twenty books for young readers. Her books are frequently selected by the Canadian Children's Book Center for their annual "Our Choice" guide to the best books published in Canada. Many have been nominated for local and national awards, including the Sheila Egoff Children's Literature Prize, the Diamond Willow Award, and the Ontario Library Association Forest of Reading Red Cedar Award.

Becky has written two popular series as well – the "Ellie and Max" series which takes place in Upper Canada in the 1800's and the Jeremy and the Enchanted Theater time travel series. She currently lives in Bridge Lake, BC.